A HEAD FOR AN EYE

by

I0666411

William Blackwell

A Head for an Eye

Copyright © **2016** WILLIAM BLACKWELL PUBLISHING. All rights reserved. This book is a work of fiction. Names, characters, places and incidents are products of the author's imagination or are used fictitiously and are not to be construed as real. Any resemblance to actual events, locales, organizations, or persons, living or dead, is entirely coincidental. No part of this book may be used or reproduced in any manner whatsoever without written permission from William Blackwell Publishing, except in the case of brief quotations embodied in critical articles and reviews.

Cover designed by Telemachus Press LLC
Published by Telemachus Press LLC
Paperback ISBN: 978-1-7389714-4-2
Version: 2016.12.01

Acknowledgements

Heartfelt thanks to my loyal and supportive friends and family, the hardworking staff at Telemachus Press, and my editor. Special thanks to the Government of Prince Edward Island for its financial support.

A Head for an Eye

Use every man according to his desert and who should 'scape whipping?
—William Shakespeare

Prologue

If violence had a foul odor, Jesus Villareal would have smelled it.

His twenty-two-year-old senses were finely tuned as he sipped corn beer in a run-down shack just outside the small town of Guadalupe y Calvo in the state of Chihuahua, northern Mexico.

He wouldn't overdo it tonight, even though his father Audiel, a Tarahumara Indian, had been known to drink gallons of the potent brew in one sitting, only to awake remarkably refreshed the next morning and run more than a hundred miles through the treacherous Sierra Madre terrain.

That was then.

This was now.

After the family farm had been seized by a Mexican drug cartel with an agenda to grow marijuana and opium, Audiel had gotten a subsistence job as a construction laborer in Mexico City. And Jesus's mother Esperanza was probably standing at a busy traffic intersection in Chihuahua City right now, hocking handcrafted baskets for a pittance.

Their traditional and simple way of life was no more.

So Jesus had ventured into Guadalupe y Calvo to integrate himself into the town of about 10,000 people. Doing odd jobs, he had saved enough money for a shoeshine kit and most afternoons he spent in the town square hustling up shoeshine jobs. But the competition was fierce, and one young man, Rodriguez Sanchez, was intent on driving him out of what he viewed as his territory.

Earlier today, Jesus had a confrontation. Rodriguez, two years his junior, threatened Jesus with physical violence if he didn't leave. Jesus adamantly refused, claiming he had as much right to make a living as anyone else.

But it was a few minutes later, when Rodriguez returned with three friends, that Jesus thought better of his resistance. After being roughed up a little, Jesus picked up his small wooden box of shoeshine accoutrements, placed it into a colorful hand-woven knapsack, and sprinted off down the road, knowing the boys would know better than to give chase. They knew enough about Jesus to realize he could outrun them in a heartbeat.

It was in his genes.

He took another sip of corn beer—*tesguino*, as it was known—and brought his gaze to the corrugated tin rusted walls, dirt floors, and the small infant crawling around in the squalor. Cooking utensils cluttered one corner and sleeping bags, blankets and pillows were bunched up in another corner. He shared the ramshackle building with Adoracion, a kindly woman of eighty-two, and the infant boy, Raphael, whom she had found abandoned on the street and adopted.

Adoracion had welcomed Jesus into her improvised abode and he did what he could to provide food and protection for the two.

It might be squalor to some, but it was home-sweet-home to Jesus and, other than Gloria, the love of his life, it was the only support group he had right now. He vowed to make the best of it.

He took another sip of the home-made brew from the dented tin cup, set it down on the makeshift table, stood up and picked up Raphael. The infant's eyes opened wide and his small toothless mouth formed an adorable smile. The baby uttered some incomprehensible gibberish as Jesus set him down on the ruffled sleeping bags, fetched a bottle, filled it with milk and stuck it into his expectant mouth. Raphael curled into a fetal position, giggled and sucked on the bottle contentedly.

The precariously hanging wooden plank door suddenly burst off its hinges and flew into the small room, landing with a crash and blowing up a small cloud of dust. The much taller Rodriguez wasted no time. He dove at Jesus, sending him crashing into the wooden table. Its fragile wooden legs collapsed under the weight of the two as a three-gallon glass container of *tesguino* rolled off and landed on Rodriguez, bubbling out on his back and legs. It rolled onto the floor and lodged on a wooden chair leg, gurgling forth its contents.

Rodriguez pummeled Jesus repeatedly in the face with tightly clenched fists—five, six, seven hard blows.

Wide-eyed, baby Raphael sucked on the milk bottle and watched.

His world growing gray, Jesus frantically stretched his left arm out, reaching for something, anything, to save his life. He found the tool of his salvation in a weathered chunk of broken wood that had once served as a table leg. He clenched it and, with strength rapidly draining, swung it at the angry head of Rodriguez.

Thwack, thwack.

A rusty nail protruding from the impromptu weapon sliced a two-inch gash along the side of Rodriguez's temple.

Rodriguez stopped for a moment, wiping a hand over the fresh blood and examining it with narrowing eyes.

Blood dripped into Jesus's eyes. He didn't know how much of it was his own and how much of it flowed from his attacker. And he didn't have time to figure it out. He bucked his hips, at the same time rolling to one side. Rodriguez grabbed his shirt, tearing it from his back as Jesus stood up, reached into his pocket and produced a small pen-knife. He flicked open the blade and waved it in a circular motion as Rodriguez scrambled to his feet, his left hand still cupped to the bleeding head wound.

A cut above Jesus's left eye was oozing blood down his nose and into both eyes, obscuring vision already impaired by the concussive blows.

"Get out of here ... or I'll kill you," Jesus said, advancing a step.

Rodriguez reached down for a chunk of wood and was interrupted by a shout. "Get out of my house now and leave him alone." It was Adoracion, standing in the sunlit doorway, a brightly-colored smock draping her fragile frame. Her aged eyes were intently focused, belying her years.

Raphael pierced the momentary silence with a deafening cry.

Rodriguez glanced at the child.

Adoracion picked up a cast-iron frying pan and stepped forward.

His head beginning to clear slightly, Jesus's confidence grew. He advanced and raised the knife high in the air.

Rodriguez glanced at the incoming threat and sprinted for the open doorway, bumping Adoracion on the way out. He sprinted down the run-down street, yelping dogs trailing his exit.

******

The next afternoon, his dark-skinned face swollen, cut and bruised from the beating, Jesus casually approached Rodriguez in the small town square as dozens of locals went about their daily grind.

In the middle of a shoeshine, Rodriguez looked up in surprise at his uninvited guest.

Jesus extracted a .45 caliber pistol and calmly squeezed the trigger three times—*kaplow, kaplow, kaplow*—the bullets penetrating Rodriguez's head.

As onlookers screamed, and Rodriguez slumped to the pavement, a pool of blood snaking out around him, Jesus nonchalantly inserted the pistol in the crotch of his jeans, turned and walked down the street.

A single thought occurred to Jesus Villareal:

This isn't murder. It's self-defense.

Chapter One

"It's self-defense. They've backed me into a corner," Matt Green said, staring at the legal document.

"Although they've done it illegally, they have indeed backed you into a corner," Sarah Walker agreed. "And, yes ... you should defend yourself."

Matt held a civil court judgment for $30,000 that Able Property Management had just won. Only problem was, the company had won the judgment through illegal and dishonest methods. Matt, a real estate investor and consultant, had fired Able for incompetence. Rod Badrickis, a partner in the company, had decided to sue Matt for meddling in Able's affairs. Additionally, Able was refusing to release another $12,000 of Matt's money, much of it tenant security deposits.

The lawsuit was a creative work of fiction. While Matt was away on a four-day holiday, Able had its lawyers serve Matt's office with an order to appear in court, which Matt never received due to the holiday. Able then sent its lawyer to court and won a judgment essentially because the accused was a no-show.

Now, through no fault of his own, Matt was out of pocket $12,000 and owed an additional $30,000—a debt he knew would get registered on his credit report, scarring his stellar credit rating. And he was stretching his credit cards as it was to make mortgage payments, never mind what Sarah's fee would be to make the problem go away—if his lawyer could even win the lawsuit.

Sarah sat at her desk on the fifth floor of a downtown Vancouver office building and waited until the vein bulging in his neck had shrunk somewhat. Knowing she would never see it disappear entirely, at least not under these conditions, she continued: "They can't legally withhold tenant security deposits, for one. Two, legally they have to serve you in person if you're being sued. We can prove you never received or signed for any paperwork. That judgment is not legal."

Matt ran a hand through his long black wavy hair and stared out the window at the gray November rain pelting down. He fought back an urge to curse. "It looks pretty legal to me."

She shuffled some files, shifted in the chair and crossed a leg. Her black business suit, crisp white blouse, and black-framed glasses projected an air of intelligence and authority. The large oak desk was stacked high with neatly organized files. "I should be able to get it overturned."

Matt scratched the four o'clock stubble on his chin. He hadn't slept much in the last two days since receiving news of the judgment. Underneath his black windbreaker, the misaligned collar of a wrinkled yellow shirt poked out. At least the jacket was zipped most of the way up. He hoped it concealed his recent apathy regarding clean laundry. "Should be able to get it overturned?"

Sarah pushed her glasses up the bridge of her small nose and focused her sea-blue eyes on Matt. "It's always a crap shoot with civil litigation—heck, litigation of any kind. But I think we've got a good shot at getting it overturned, and getting most of your money back—at least the tenant damage deposits."

Matt sighed. It would have to do. Not only was he getting ripped off for money owed to him, but now he had a $30,000 judgment hanging over his head. What a fucked-up justice system. Anyone could sue anyone for anything. Right or wrong, they probably would have a 50-50 chance of winning, better if they had money and resources. He remembered a story a lawyer friend had relayed about a family of East Indians living in Vancouver whose only employment was driving around every day instigating vehicular collisions, then suing for personal injury and other damages. Apparently they lived in an estate area of the city and were thriving. Throw enough shit against the wall and some of it's bound to stick.

"What sort of plan of attack do you suggest?" he asked, scratching a belly that two years ago looked more like a six-pack than a spare tire.

Sarah glanced at her notes, scribbled something on a steno pad, shuffled a few papers in the file and looked at Matt, a smile barely forming at the edges of her full and pouty lips. "Well, at this point I think we should go on the offensive. Get the judgment overturned, get the tenant deposits returned and counter-sue."

Matt thought about it. He wanted his pound of flesh for sure. But at what cost? If Sarah got the judgment overturned, the tenant deposits returned, wouldn't a counter-suit drag on for a long time and become costly? And who would win? Only the lawyers? "Let's take steps one and two first. I'll think about the third step if and when we win rounds one and two. Steps one and two are merely self-defense."

"Sounds reasonable," Sarah said with a finality that suggested the meeting was over.

Matt was glad for it. Even though he found her attractive, time with her was money, and money he didn't have.

She accompanied him to the door. "Don't worry. I've won ninety-eight per cent of my cases. I feel good about this one."

A few minutes later, rain-drenched at the wheel of his black Toyota Supra (he had forgotten his umbrella), Matt felt hot rage boiling up inside him, the large vein in his neck growing and pulsing. He looked in the mirror at his reddening face with slits for eyes and frowned, seeing another vein snaking across his creased forehead.

He knew it was all Rod Badrickis's doing. If he saw the man on the street now, he thought he might leap out of the car and choke him to death. Until this moment, he never realized he harbored the capacity for murder. *Don't be stupid. You don't have the guts. You're not capable of murder.*

Chapter Two

I could murder him. I could just kill him. Angelique Augusto had typed the email and now her finger rested on the send button. *Should I send it?* She slowly removed her finger, stood up, and paced around her modest one-bedroom rented apartment on Denman Street, Vancouver, British Columbia.

She walked over to the window and gazed out. It was dusk and rain pelted the streets from the gray sky. People holding umbrellas walked hurriedly past and vehicles swished along on puddled streets. White noise. There was always white noise on Denman Street, a hub of coffee shops, bars, restaurants, boutique specialty shops and the like, located in the downtown core within walking distance to Stanley Park and the beach.

She returned to her computer at a black utilitarian workstation in a corner of the living room, sat down and read her unsent email. *Is it such a torture for you to talk to me? You don't return my text messages or emails. Am I that hard to look at or deal with that you can't respond?*

She hesitated for a second, sighed, clicked the send button and stared at the screen, her stomach knotting in anxiety. *What did I just do? He's going to think I'm a psycho.* But it was too late. When he got around to it, Matt Green would be reading the message and probably wondering what he had gotten himself into using the dating site Plenty of Fish. Hell, he might think it should be more appropriately called Plenty of Freaks.

But Angelique didn't look like a freak, if such a stereotype even existed. At five-foot-ten, with long shapely legs, a curvaceous butt, melon-shaped 44-DD breasts and flat stomach, she turned a lot of male heads strolling down the street. Turned a lot of heads in the downtown accounting firm, where she worked as a secretary. And her body wasn't all men were looking at. She had a thick, curly mane of black hair that flowed all the way down her back, covering half of the perfect curvature of her buttocks. She had smooth, olive-toned skin, black penetrating eyes, thin black eyebrows, a small nose, pouty lips and small, straight white teeth.

She thought her breasts were too big. But Matt had assured her on the third date he had a thing for big breasts. "Whatever you do, don't reduce them," he said, fondling them with a satisfied smile. "They're beautiful just the way they are. And the melon shape is perfect. I love them."

At twenty-five, Angelique was fifteen years Matt's junior. During one of their many internet chat conversations prior to meeting, she had asked him what he thought of the age difference, to which he had typed: *Age is just a number in your head. It only bothers you if you let it. It doesn't bother me. I'm lucky that way I guess.*

She had responded: *I definitely think you're lucky to have a woman as young as me. LOL.*

But Angelique wasn't laughing out loud now. It had been two days since she had spoken to Matt. Although they had only been dating for a few weeks, she was madly in love with him. And maybe he was just trying to placate her, but in one of his email responses he had ended it with *I love you,* to her ten that ended with either *I love you or love, Angelique.*

Angelique stood up, pacing, wrapping her long hair into a pony-tail that she neatly tied with an elastic band and black stone brooch. *What the hell do I do? How do I handle this relationship? Maybe I should just break up with him before he breaks up with me.*

In that crazy moment, gripped by the often-irrational forces of love or what Angelique perceived as love, it never dawned on her that maybe what she was looking for was a father figure.

Growing up in San Agustinillo, Mexico, she could hardly call her father a loving man. One of eight children crammed into a small two-bedroom house, she had taken her fair share of beatings at Edgardo's hands. It still brought tears to her eyes when she remembered him slapping, punching and kicking her, and on one occasion, chasing her down the street, seizing her long hair, dragging her to the ground, and pounding on her with savage fists to the cackling laughter of cruel, insensitive neighborhood boys.

She thought her mother, Alicia, was simply a victim for allowing the beatings of her children. Alicia was too scared to speak up. After suffering physical and psychological abuse at Edgardo's hands, Alicia decided to keep quiet at his cruel discipline of their children.

At an early age, Angelique realized she didn't fit into the family. She didn't resemble her mother, father, or any of the other siblings. She had asked her father one day if she had been adopted. His eyes had narrowed instantly before a swinging left arm had delivered a hard backhand to the side of her face.

She had recovered physically from the strike, but questions remained. Were these her real parents? Had she been adopted? After the vicious response to her query, she wouldn't dare utter the question ever again. But the nagging question created a hardened resolve to leave her unsavory upbringing.

At the age of sixteen, Angelique vowed to do everything in her power to get away from that awful situation. After six mentally and physically abusive relationships with machismo Mexican men—in one case, she had been beaten so badly she had been fortunate to escape with her life—she turned to the massive power and scope of the internet.

At the age of twenty-two, she met a Canadian man, Greg Loewen, on a dating website. He visited her in Mexico twice, they fell in love, married and eventually moved to Vancouver. But then Greg, twenty-five years Angelique's senior, rapidly started losing interest in the relationship. He accused Angelique of being impetuous, childish, immature, and someone who had "the potential to turn into a fucking stalker. You want to control me and know what I'm doing every second that I'm away from you. That's why you call, text or email twenty times a day. You don't trust me. And without trust, what the fuck do we have, anyway?"

The proverbial straw that broke the camel's back was the fact she had kept her accounts up with internet dating sites. While Greg worked, she trolled the web looking for someone perhaps just a little better. One night, she had accidentally left five windows to different sites open and Greg had stumbled upon them.

It seemed like old habits die hard, Angelique thought sadly as she returned to the computer and opened the profile of a Toronto "real estate mogul" who had just sent her a message expressing interest. She grimaced as soon as she read it: *You're hot, honey. Fuck me. I'd like to fondle your beautiful breasts. Get back ASAP baby.*

Grinding her teeth, eyes narrowing, she immediately typed *Fuck you, you pervert*, reported the email to the website administration as inappropriate and blocked the user from further contact.

She closed Plenty of Fish, Latin American Cupid, Lavalife, and craigslist personals—a fraction of the dating websites she frequented—and powered down the computer. She hastily checked her smart phone to see if Matt had responded, frowned when she noticed he had not, pulled on a long black coat, grabbed her umbrella and left. A café latte at the local Starbucks was what she wanted. Maybe it was time to start meeting men in the flesh instead of on stupid dating sites. Dating websites attracted all manner of psychos, perverts and freaks.

Walking into the Starbucks, a man reading a newspaper ogled Angelique as she approached the counter. Angelique smiled at him, ordered a latte, and thought of what she would say to Matt when he called. *I'm going to break up with him. I'll tell him it's been fun but I can't handle this kind of neglect, something like that. Maybe say he's just a bad person for making me fall in love with him. Tell him the dream has turned into a nightmare.*

Chapter Three

This is a nightmare, Matt thought, stopped at a red light in congested traffic on the way into his office the following morning. It was a gray and drizzly day. He stared at the email from Angelique on his smart phone. *Is it such a torture for you to talk to me?* What the hell was that? They hadn't been dating for three weeks, and Angelique was acting like they had been married for ten years, maybe just starting what would turn into a nasty divorce. They had slept together, what, twice?

Matt thought there were some red flags at the beginning that he had conveniently chosen to ignore, perhaps because of his obsession with mammoth mammary glands. When they had started to chat online, Angelique had called him a liar about five sentences into the conversation, after Matt had complimented her on what he viewed as decent prose. It wasn't even an attempt at flattery, really, just an observation that she had a very good command of the English language for someone who had lived most of her life in Mexico. Her response had shocked him: *You're lying to me. You're just saying that to make me feel good.*

Wow! We don't even know each other and already I'm a liar. Trust issues. What happens when we get to know each other? Matt thought.

There were other things as well. She had started to end the chat sessions with *I love you* after two or three rather short chats.

And there were the troublesome queries of late. Emails that said: *Where are you? Who are you with? When are you coming home? Would you mind telling me?* Other variations of the same theme: *Where were you? Who were you with?* And the one that had scared him the most: *I want to know where you are at all times. You need to report to me.*

But hadn't he encouraged at least the intimacy—on and offline—frothing at the mouth while viewing her profile pictures that displayed abundant cleavage? He had been dying to get her in the sack. And when he finally had, the experience was nothing short of miraculous.

But truth be told, Matt wasn't sure he wanted a serious relationship right now. He had too many financial problems and jumping on the capitalist treadmill appealed to his need—or greed—to prove himself through the acquisition of material wealth. He found the pursuit of material gain much more satisfying than any relationship could be. At least with capitalism, you were rewarded for your calculated efforts. In relationships, that wasn't always the case. Your girlfriend could run off at any time with a man she thought had more attributes than you, maybe even meet someone on Facebook with a nicer looking mug than yours.

And he didn't put it past Angelique to be one of those types. But, at the same time, he was confused about her intentions. She clung to him. She needed him. She doted on him. She wanted to know what he was doing every second of every day. *Isn't that the recipe for a stalker? Or a control freak?* She sent him love letters with little pictures of hearts, couples strolling arm-in-arm, kissing, watching a sunset, or in some other romantic repose.

And when he looked into her intently focused eyes, he saw pure love. It seemed insane she could fall in love with him in such a short time. But was it really that insane? What about love at first sight? There were people falling in love every second all over the world, Matt supposed, many of them at first sight.

And when she didn't hear back from him immediately, she would instantly begin to worry that it was over and send him messages like: *I haven't heard back from you in an hour and I want to hear from you before I go to bed; tell me you love me so I can have a good night. I'm sad because I think you don't love me anymore.* ☹

Some men might think her completely wacked and end the relationship immediately. It was crazy, but all the attention endeared her to Matt. It was nice to be loved, nice to be needed, nice to be thought about all the time, nice to come home to his apartment knowing that he had a "last call" to make before going to bed—a last call to someone who held him fondly in a very exclusive neighborhood of her heart. *Is that what this is?*

And Matt thought he understood Angelique. They had something in common. Angelique had briefly told Matt about the abuse and rejection at her father's cruel hands. Although she had grown up in a relatively poor family and Matt had been raised in an upper-middle class family in the upmarket Kitsilano area of West Vancouver, his father, a successful pharmaceutical sales rep, and his mother, a top realtor, never had a whole lot of time for Matt, his younger brother Jeff, or his younger sister Daria. They just weren't around enough to pay a lot of attention to their kids. His parents had a point to prove, and it had a lot to do with how many toys and how much money they could accumulate—buying into the capitalist machine and The American Dream.

As a result, Matt took rejection hard. He remembered his last long-term relationship, which had ended ten years ago. Sheila was everything to him: smart, attractive, a great sense of humor, and very ambitious. She wrote columns for *The Vancouver Sun* and was an active member of the Greenpeace party—she even ran for a member of parliament in a federal election.

And she loved him dearly.

When Matt hadn't heard from Sheila for a few hours, he would go off the deep end, worrying, wondering what she was doing. Eventually, his insecurity overwhelmed him. He spent two days crafting what he thought was a well-worded I'm-dumping-you email, then agonized at his computer for six hours before finally pushing the send button. Five minutes later, Sheila, who had not yet read the email, phoned him. He saw her number flash and didn't dare answer. Her message still reverberated in his mind: *Matt, it's me. I know you have a birthday coming up and I was going to make it a big surprise party, but I changed my mind. I decided just the two of us could do something special together. I want you to come over for dinner and then I have a very special surprise. And, yes, it's romantic. Call me when you have a chance. I love you.*

The one that got away. The one he regretted losing.

Wasn't Angelique behaving almost exactly the same way he had, for essentially the same reasons? He was sure she was. They had *that* in common. Angelique didn't know it, but Matt understood her emotions. Matt remembered what his shrink had said: "Because you didn't get enough love as a child—for all intents and purposes you were abandoned by your parents—your concept of love is through obedience, obligation, fear and guilt trips. And whatever Sheila did wouldn't have been enough for you. You would continue to seek love from others, scared that you would never really be able to love her, or you don't deserve her love. It's an unhealthy perception of love, that someone is obligated to love you. And to put them under that obligation you try and control them. A symptom of the borderline personality disorder is you become a control freak."

Control freak? Isn't that text-book Angelique? "Fuck it," he said. He didn't want to think about it right now. And outside of those tantalizingly large melons, the only thing Matt wanted to think about was making money and exacting revenge on Able Property Management. That fucker Rod Badrickis was going to pay for his underhanded and illegal tactics.

By the time his thoughts returned to the busy Georgia and Robson Street intersection, honking horns were sounding off from behind. A disgruntled, red-faced motorist rolled down a window and yelled, "Wake up, you fucking idiot. Can't you see the fucking light is green?" The angry bald man punctuated his poetry with a one-finger salute. Matt rolled down the window of his Supra, obliged the greeting by flashing his middle finger, and accelerated.

He heard it before he saw it.

Thunk ... thunk!

A cyclist slammed into the front left fender of his Supra, the momentum propelling rider over handlebars. He landed on the hood splayed out on his back.

Matt slammed on the brakes, put the car in park and climbed out. The young man wore a full-body black spandex suit and a red crash helmet. He slowly picked himself off the hood.

"Are you okay?" Matt asked.

"What the fuck are you doing, running a red light?" the cyclist said, standing up. He noticed his right elbow was cut and bleeding. He was tall and skinny with a red goatee, tattooed arms and piercings in his nose and ears. He had a black cylindrical tube-style knapsack slung over his shoulder—the mark of a downtown corporate courier.

"That light wasn't red," Matt said, although he wondered about the veracity of his own words. But he certainly wasn't stupid enough to admit anything. "It was green. You ran into me. Are you okay?"

"I ... don't know," the courier said, lifting his bike up and frowning at the bent front rim.

Other than a few scratches, one on the torn right knee of his spandex suit, he looked none the worse for wear.

The last thing Matt wanted was more litigation, even though he thought he was in the right. The courier had hit him, not the other way around. But like Sarah had pointed out, when it came to courtroom litigation it was a crap shoot—a complicated system that often did not err on the side of justice. A stage of smoke and mirrors, posturing and posing, actors and acting that was often far-removed from truth.

"Why don't we settle this with some cash?" Matt asked. Cars were now at a standstill at the busy intersection. Disgruntled drivers honked horns while others rolled down their windows and filmed the drama on their smart phones.

It would probably end up on Facebook or You Tube and who knew what other social media.

"Here's a card," Matt said. "I'm going to pull onto Robson Street and park. Meet me over there." The courier nodded. Matt parked, exited, and the courier approached.

Just then, another car screeched to a stop in the middle of Robson Street, and a man climbed out.

Matt's eyes widened. It was the bald, red-faced man who had so cordially offered a one-finger salute earlier. Matt didn't have a chance to react.

"Flip me the bird, will you, motherfucker?" Baldy slammed a left hook into Matt's chin, followed by a right cross to the eye. Matt dropped to the road like a sack of rocks. He felt cold raindrops falling on his face and into his eyes as the gray light of day faded to black.

Chapter Four

"It's only a black eye. You'll live," Salomo Abramsson said the next afternoon in Matt's downtown condo. The upscale fifteenth-floor two-bedroom unit had a panoramic view of the city, False Creek and Stanley Park. The gray sky pelted rain onto traffic, buildings and pedestrians below.

After the knock-out blows, Matt had woken up a few minutes later dazed and confused, helped to his feet by some good Samaritans and watched by curious bystanders. He had exchanged contact details with Joe Andreas, the young courier, who said: "You'll be hearing from me."

He had called his secretary, Michelle Anderson, telling her to cancel all his investment consultations for the day. He would be going home to bed. He had thought about going to the hospital for a check-up to insure his head was functioning normally, but had dismissed the thought soon afterward. He hated hospitals almost as much as he disliked doctors. So he had gone home to Wall Centre, taken the elevator up to the fifteenth floor, popped four Tylenol Extra-Strength pills and gone to bed.

He awoke slightly less groggy at seven the next morning to three voicemails, three text messages and three emails from Angelique. He called and agreed to meet her in a few hours at Sorento Coffee Shop, located on the main floor of Wall Centre. She said she had some urgent news.

Matt had again cancelled his appointments for the day. His clients would just have to wait. Matt was sure he was suffering from a mild concussion.

After showering, he had called Sal to discuss the accident with the courier. He wanted a professional opinion on how to handle it.

Now they sat in Matt's contemporary living room, drinking coffee. It was painted in dark green tones and furnished with black leather couches, hand-made slate and rod iron coffee and end tables. Colorful abstract art hung on the walls. Matt had just explained the accident to Sal and groaned, rubbing his eye. "I know I'll live, but my fucking head still hurts," he said to his friend of five years.

"Well, just take it easy for the day. Don't push yourself like you always do," Sal said. He sat in a leather armchair, the picture of class, intelligence and sophistication with his $10,000 black suit, crisply-starched white shirt and bold red tie. To Sal, the red tie was a symbolic mind-fuck for his clients. Many of them came to him in the red. The tie reinforced that and reminded them of why they needed the corporate lawyer's expert services. Sal specialized in setting up tax shelters for the wealthy and those on the brink of financial ruin. He also wrote government business legislation. He had a wealth of contacts in the private and public sector, and his services were in high demand.

Sal had done a short stint as a criminal lawyer, but what he perceived as timidity had pushed him into corporate law. He didn't think he was cut from cloth tough enough to face down judge, jury and crown prosecutor in a public courtroom. For that, you needed a coat of Kevlar armor.

At 55, Sal could easily pass for 35. He worked out in the gym regularly, only occasionally went on alcoholic benders, and watched his diet like a Weight Watchers member. He had close-cropped sandy brown hair, high cheekbones and chiseled features. He was a well-travelled playboy who occasionally took sex-vacation sojourns and slept with multiple women over a one or two-week period. Matt twice had accompanied Sal on said lascivious adventures.

"I have to meet Angelique," Matt said. "She has something urgent to tell me."

Sal's brow crinkled. He had been kept up to date on Matt's recent made-on-the-internet union and did not approve. "We'll get to Angelique in a minute. Let's talk about this accident first. Have you heard from this courier yet?"

Matt shook his head.

Sal scratched his chin, sipped coffee, and stared at the gray city vista. "Tell me again what you said to him after you woke up."

"I said I don't feel well."

"What did he say?"

"He said, 'Neither do I.'"

"I think he's contemplating a law suit."

"I didn't do anything."

"You say you weren't sure if the light was red, green or yellow when you entered the intersection. If he can produce witnesses—easy to do—who say the light was red when you entered, he's got you—careless or negligent driving causing bodily injury. It's your fault. And who knows what he's going to say about the severity of his injuries. But I'll guarantee you one thing—if he sues you, and he probably will, he'll be going after a minimum of $250,000. People don't sue for less anymore. It's not worth a lawyer's time to get involved. My guess is he'll be going after a lot more. At least a million."

"I didn't hit him. He hit me."

"That doesn't matter," Sal said, standing and checking his smart phone. "I have to go. But I'll give you some advice. Call him and offer a settlement. But make sure he signs a mutual general release form clearly stating he will not pursue litigation with respect to the accident—now or ever. Have your lawyer, Sarah, prepare it. And make sure his signature is notarized by his own council. You don't want him coming after you in the future claiming he didn't know what he was signing."

Matt frowned and scratched his head. He would have to call Joe before he left to meet Angelique. "How much should I offer him?"

"I don't know, start with $5,000 and work your way up."

"At what point should I tell him to go fuck himself?"

"Don't tell him that. If you don't agree with the number, stall and talk to Sarah or me about it. Always stall when you don't agree. Give yourself time to strategize." Sal knew lately Matt's business ventures were not producing fruit. In addition to Able's lawsuit, he had three recently-vacated rental properties due to the company's incompetence. He was over-leveraged on real estate acquisitions and the market had recently taken a nose-dive. It would be difficult to dump the real estate and get out of the tough spot. Matt's back was to the wall. He had to make money to service his debt or face bank foreclosure.

Matt accompanied Sal to the door. Before leaving, Sal focused his intelligent blue eyes on Matt—the litigator stare, crafted to intimidate. "Listen, I don't care how many love letters Angelique has sent you." Sal had already reviewed Angelique's profile online. In time, he would send her a solicitation and test her loyalty to Matt. "She could send that text to anybody. For all you know, it's scripted. She doesn't love you. She wants your money, which she thinks you have. With your experience, you should know better. You're not excused by lack of experience. If you think she's in love with you, no offense, but you should seriously question your judgment."

Matt didn't know whether to thank Sal or punch him in the face. "You're entitled to your opinion. I'm not entitled to agree with it."

Closing the door, Matt frowned. Maybe Sal was right. But he felt like he had been smashed in an already-aching head by a high-speed cannonball.

******

Matt waited twenty-eight minutes in Sorento, nervously chewing on the plastic lip of his take-out coffee cup. Other patrons drank coffee and chatted. Cars swished by in puddles outside while pedestrians walked by, or ran to escape the downpour.

Matt worried about what Angelique's emergency was. She was late, but that wasn't unusual for her. She operated on Mexican time, which differed from Pacific Daylight time by as much as an hour and a half, in her case.

Matt had called the courier prior to leaving and left a message asking him to "please call me at your earliest convenience to discuss the accident." He had no idea how it was going to play out, but wanted to get it resolved and off his chest soon.

To kill time, he checked email on his smart phone. He noticed a new message from Sal and opened it. He frowned while reading it: *I must say, I will add; this is just too much for me. I don't know what to say really. I think the question of whether Angelique is in love with you is just complete and utter bullshit on your part. But like you stated, it's your call and your life, of course. Now I got that one off my chest. I am not trying to insult you even if I'm being very blunt and rude. Have a good one. Cheers!*

Cannonball number two rocked Matt's precarious grip on his emotions, as if the first one wasn't enough. Anger flushed his face. Maybe he liked Angelique more than he was ready to admit. *Fucking asshole. What the fuck does he know about relationships? A sex tourist—that's all he is. I could punch him in the fucking head, hiding behind email; doesn't have the stones to tell me to my face.*

The glass coffee shop door swung open and Angelique appeared, closing a black umbrella and dropping it into a nearby umbrella holder. She looked flustered, her eyes bloodshot and watery. It was clear she had been crying. Francis, the owner, ogled her from his perch at the cash register and smiled at Matt with an approving glance. Very nice.

She ordered a black coffee and sat down next to Matt at the window-front table. "What happened to your eye?" she asked.

"Road rage. Some nut punched me in the face."

"Are you okay?"

"A mild concussion, I think."

"Do you know who did this?"

"No, he took off. No one's come forward with any details so far."

"That's terrible."

Matt nodded. He wanted to move on. He felt a stirring in his loins. Angelique's presence, her love letters and even her voice often had that physiological effect on him. During the initial days of the courtship, he had walked around with a permanent hard-on. "I'm sorry I didn't get back to you earlier. I've been a little stressed out lately."

Angelique frowned. Matt wondered if he had picked the right venue. A few conversations stopped and eyes stared at the couple, as if waiting for a melodramatic scene from the soap opera, *As the World Turns*, to unfold. In this case, it was more like *As the Stomach Turns*.

Angelique pointed to a quieter table in a far corner. "Do you mind if we sit over there?"

Matt nodded and they changed seats, he hoped out of earshot of other patrons. Francis shot him a sideways glance. Trouble?

Angelique removed the lid from her coffee and stared at the black swirl for a few seconds. She slowly brought a lovesick gaze to Matt's eyes. "Do you know what this is about?"

"You're pissed off because I didn't get back to you right away."

"Maybe I'm a little pissed, but I'm more hurt than anything. All that stuff you said about how you love me. It's just words. You have your own plans, your own goals and they don't include me."

"I don't understand. We've only just started seeing each other."

Angelique wiped her right eye, glanced around the coffee shop, and looked at Matt seriously. "It doesn't matter if you understand. Not now. Don't you know I'm head-over-heels in love with you? But love is just a psychological drug, it's worse than being sick. It makes you worse. Us, what are we really—a lethal cocktail?"

"Honey, I didn't know the rules. I didn't know I had to get back to you right away."

"What do you think love is ... something you can play with? Do you think you can play with my emotions? Or do you just like my big boobs?" She had raised her voice and a few more heads turned toward them.

"You told me you love me. I told you the same," Matt said.

"Why, because you thought that's what I wanted to hear?"

Matt was becoming confused. His aching head and the recent cannonballs from Sal weren't helping matters. "No, I felt it at the time."

"You're a liar, Matt. You've been playing with my emotions. And that's just a cruel thing to do to someone. You want the truth?"

Matt had a feeling he was going the truth according to Angelique whether he wanted it or not.

"You and I are nothing. That's the truth. It doesn't matter. Not much passed between us. In time, I'll get over you." She stood, leaving the coffee untouched. Matt half-expected her to pick it up and chuck the contents into his face. Instead, she said: "I know your plans don't include me. You don't really want me. You don't know what you want. I wish you all the success in your life. I wish you the best."

"Wait ... wait."

But Angelique stormed out of the coffee shop, rubbernecking patron eyes following her exit-stage-left.

Matt hung his head for a few minutes after she left, ignoring the customer's glances. He didn't know if it was the worst moment of his life or a blessing in disguise. He had to admit, in some ways she was right. He didn't know what he wanted. If he knew, would Angelique be his downfall? Was he just an obsession to her? Did she have the potential to become a dangerous stalker? Or was she his soulmate? When it came to affairs of the heart, Matt considered himself a novice. He didn't have a clue.

But thinking about it brought more confusion to an already-muddled mind. His phone rang just as he stood to leave. Recognizing the courier's phone number, Matt grimaced. *Shit, maybe another lawsuit to add insult to injury.*

Chapter Five

"It's a small injury," Jesus said as Gloria Alvarez traced her index finger over a small cut above his right eyebrow. "I heal fast. I'm tough."

Jesus wasn't exaggerating. The Tarahumara have been called the toughest race on Earth, outrunning the world's best and most highly-trained long-distance runners on a diet and lifestyle far from technologically-advanced. They eat fruit, beans, yams, whole grains, vegetables and a lot of corn. They rarely eat meat, smoke tobacco heavily and have been known to party hard and often on potent corn beer until all hours of the night.

They are a peaceful, spiritual and mysterious race of people who live off the land in one of the most treacherous and unforgiving landscapes in the world—the Sierra Madre in Chihuahua state, Mexico. Living in small cabins, cliff overhangs or caves, they use oxen to plow their fields, grow corn, squash and beans and stockpile food for the winter.

Without modern amenities or high-tech communication devices, these skilled craftsmen are the personification of a simple way of life, juxtaposed with humankind's desire to accumulate material wealth, complicate our lives with high-tech communication devices, and become wholly absorbed in the often petty stresses and concerns of modern-day society.

With a population of about 70,000, the Tarahumara have a difficult existence. Their average life span is forty-five years and their traditional way of life is constantly under attack from legal and illegal exploitative forces.

Carl Sophus Lumholtz, a Norwegian explorer, spent nearly three years living among the Tarahumara in the 1890s. He writes:

> *The Tarahumara in his native condition is many times better off, morally, mentally, and economically, than his civilized brother: but the white man will not let him alone as long as he has anything worth taking away. Only those who by dear experience have learned to be cautious are able to maintain themselves independently; but such cases are becoming more and more rare.*

> *It is the same old story over again, in America, as in Africa and Asia, and everywhere. The simple-minded native is made the victim of the progressive white, who, by fair means or foul, deprives him of his country. Luckily, withal, the Tarahumara has not yet been wiped out of existence. His blood is fused into the working classes of Mexico, and he grows a Mexican. But it may take a century yet before they will all be made the servants of whites and disappear ... Their assimilation may benefit Mexico, but one may well ask: Is it just? Must the weaker always be first crushed, before he can be assimilated by the new condition of things?*

But, more than a hundred years later, the Tarahumara has not been wiped out. They still live a largely traditional existence, dogged and determined to maintain their way of life. Although they are a peaceful people who have been called the kindest and happiest on the planet, they are also known to be ferocious warriors when thrust into a battle to preserve their culture. Early Spanish conquistadors found out the hard way when they invaded in the 16th century that the Tarahumara can be a deadly force to be reckoned with when their traditional way of life is threatened.

The indigenous Indians retreated into their unforgiving terrain where the conquistadors could not follow. After getting killed off in sniper and ambush fashion—in one case, Spanish decapitated heads were impaled on spears to drive home a deterrent message—the Spanish explorers finally retreated and abandoned the attack.

Currently, the Tarahumara traditional existence is under attack by the drug trade and the ruthless violence and exploitation that accompanies it. The Sierra Madre Occidental—the Mother Mountains of the Mexican West—is one of the most productive drug-growing regions on the planet for marijuana crops or opium seeds, the source of many narcotics. Some Tarahumara farmers are being forced to grow opium or marijuana instead of corn.

According to website Borderland Beat, "Stories of terror in Guadalupe y Calvo Municipality, located in the Tarahumara Mountains, repeat themselves day after day, without municipal, state or federal authorities doing anything about it."

According to a September 27, 2012, Borderland Beat report: "... violence is the daily bread" in the region. Recently, a crime group "executed a young man, decapitating him in front of his relatives. Before they cut his throat, the murderers made a 16-inch cut on his chest."

Author Richard Grant (*God's Middle Finger: Into the Lawless Heart of the Sierra Madre*), who "developed an unfortunate fascination with this lawless place," describes it:

> *The rules of law and society have never taken hold in the Sierra Madre, which is home to bandits, drug smugglers, Mormons, cave-dwelling Tarahumara Indians, opium farmers, cowboys, and other assorted outcasts. Outsiders are not welcome; drugs are the primary source of income; murder is all but a regional pastime. The Mexican army occasionally goes in to burn marijuana and opium crops—the modern treasure of the Sierra Madre—but otherwise the government stays away. In its stead are the drug lords, who have made it one of the biggest drug-producing areas in the world.*

******

As he stared into his Tarahumara girlfriend's sorrowful brown eyes, Jesus wasn't thinking about the lawlessness of the Sierra Madre. To his mind, it was the law of the land, in many ways a recently-acquired law of his people. He justified his actions as a simple case of self-defense. To Jesus, it was cut and dried—an eye for an eye, or in this instance, A Head for an Eye. You fuck with me, I kill you.

Simple.

But what did sadden and disturb him as he sat on rumpled sleeping bags inside the ramshackle shack, while Adoracion watched Raphael crawl around in the litter-strewn backyard, was that he would be leaving Gloria, the woman with whom he had grown up as a little boy in the pastures, fields and caves of the Sierra Madre.

From childhood playmates, to best friends, to lovers, to soulmates—their love for one another had stood the test of time and tragedy.

Now there would be another test, perhaps the toughest of their union. Jesus would stand trial in two days, very likely get convicted of second-degree murder, and would probably be sentenced to an eight-year prison term. In his favor were the laws in the municipality of Guadalupe y Calvo. Since twelve hours in prison was considered one day served, he would likely only serve four years. But those years would be harsh—in squalid, fiercely territorial, and hierarchical conditions. To survive the horrific conditions would be a monumental accomplishment.

"Sure, you'll heal fast," Gloria said, slowly removing her finger from the wound and clasping Jesus's hand tightly. Her eyes welled up and she brushed a lock of long curly black hair from her face. "But you're going away for a long time. What am I going to do?"

Jesus had resigned himself to his fate. But Gloria's love was the one thing that truly gave him happiness and a small sense of inner peace. It was nice to be needed, admired, missed and loved. Life without Gloria would not be easy.

And Jesus was the only thing good in Gloria's life. Years ago, her parents had mounted an ill-fated protest against an organized crime group aiming to convert their cornfield to a marijuana field. For their trouble, they had been bound, gagged, led into an open field, shot in the head and buried in shallow graves. Gloria had been lucky to escape with her life. Her older sister, Angel, had disappeared from the family farmstead at the tender age of five, kidnapped or killed. Gloria didn't know to this day whether Angel was alive or dead.

The door to the shack creaked open and a uniformed police officer armed with an AK-47 assault rifle held up five fingers.

Jesus nodded and the man respectfully closed the door.

The tears Gloria had been holding back began to flow freely.

"I'm sorry," Jesus said, unable to stop the tide of emotion welling up in his throat. He hugged Gloria tightly. "I was so stupid. I should have thought of you before killing that bastard. I'm so sorry. Shit, shit, shit. It's just the laws here ... you know how it is, baby. You have to follow the laws, obey the laws. Rodriguez broke the law. I had to defend myself. I had to do it. I had no choice. Please understand. You can visit me. Maybe they'll let me go. Maybe I'll get acquitted ..."

"It doesn't matter," Gloria interrupted, pressing a wet cheek to his face. "I will love you always."

Jesus could tell by her forlorn eyes she wasn't buying his sudden optimism. "I love you. Will you wait for me?"

Gloria nodded, gave him a long, passionate kiss, withdrew, and said: "I will always wait for you. You are the one and only love of my life."

Adoracion peered in the back door, holding a giggling Raphael in her arms.

Jesus nodded and the two entered to say goodbye.

Three minutes later, a police pickup truck hauled a resolute but sad Jesus Villareal away, while Adoracion, baby Raphael and Gloria watched, waved and cried as the vehicle disappeared down the dusty dirt road.

Jesus didn't know it, but the toughest challenge of a life of desperation and despair was about to rear its terrifying head.

Chapter Six

Do you like to give head? Angelique was initially going to disconnect and block the Plenty of Fish chatter—maybe report Bob Bolder to the website administration as inappropriate—but some innate need for retribution changed her mind.

After unceremoniously dumping Matt, if you could call it that, given the short duration of their passionate but tumultuous union, she had returned to her apartment, opened up her array of dating sites, and began sending out feelers to find the man of her dreams. She knew in an hour she would be meeting Alex Liberty, the ogling executive who had recently chatted her up in Starbucks.

But, hell, she still had time for a little fun.

I do like to give head, Angelique typed. *In fact, it's my favorite. I love it.*

Bob Bolder returned the message with three smiley faces, followed by: *Wow, wow, wow. That really turns me on. Do you blow on the first date?*

Angelique typed: *Only if I like the man's cock. I hate small cocks. How big is your cock? Don't lie to me now. Tell the truth.*

I have eight inches.

Hard or soft?

Soft. Hard it's eleven inches.

I don't believe you.

It's true.

I don't believe you. All men say that. All men lie.

I'm not bullshitting. It's true.

Show me a picture.

There was a long pause between texts, as if Bob was deciding whether he could live up to the surname Bolder.

She prompted Bolder some more. She had known the fine upstanding citizen for exactly thirty minutes. Already he was talking like they had a longstanding intimate relationship, where this kind of behavior was not only tolerated but accepted, mutually enjoyed and encouraged—like sexting between consenting couples.

Angelique typed: *Do you want that blowjob or not, Bob? You show me the right cock and I'll show you a blowjob that'll blow your fucking mind. It'll rock your productive and noble life.*

She thought she had gone too far. *Shit, why the sarcasm? To hell with it, words get misunderstood all the time in chat sessions. I should be able to explain it away.*

Bolder typed: *Productive and noble life?*

Isn't that what your profile says?

You're right. I didn't think you'd remember.

I don't forget an amazing profile like that. You might be just what I'm looking for in a man.

Hang on I'll send the photo.

A few seconds later, Angelique accepted a sent image, opened it, and stared wide-eyed, swallowing a lump in her throat that made her want to gag. *Young, dumb and full of cum.* It was a close-up shot of an erect circumcised penis, a male hand tugging at the large swollen member. Bolder wasn't lying about the size.

Truth was, Angelique did enjoy giving head. It *was* her favorite thing in the world to do to a man—but certainly not this scumbag. Angelique had to be in love with a man to go down on him. And Bolder missed that mark by a longshot, although he had lived up to his surname.

She immediately emailed the image to the site administration, with a little note saying: *Bob Bolder should be banned from Plenty of Fish. Look at the perverted images he's sending out. This came to me completely unsolicited.*

She posted the image on her Tumblr page with a warning about its origin. She also uploaded the image to Facebook and posted a link to it in the Plenty of Fish forum, Lavalife and craigslist personals. Just for fun, she uploaded a short video on You Tube and added the link to a few other dating site discussion forums.

Bolder typed: *Well, was I lying?*

No, you weren't lying. But, just so you know, I've sent the image to Plenty of Fish administration and plastered it all over the web with a warning to stay the fuck away from Bob Bolder. It's a good thing you hide behind a pseudonym, you fucking pervert. Otherwise you'd have the cops banging on your door—you internet sexual predator freak. Your trolling days are over. Thanks again for your interest and fuck you very much.

Before he could respond, she blocked him, deleted his profile from her favorites list, and logged off the website.

Angelique smiled, but only briefly. At one time, she took great satisfaction in luring sexual predators out of their safe zones, blacklisting them on the internet, even reporting them to police. But now, not so much. She was still upset over the break-up with Matt. Perhaps she had been too rough on him. He had looked a mess. It was obvious he had been having a bad week—accidents, road rage, lawsuits, financial problems. All she had done was make matters worse.

Poor Matt.

She frowned slightly as she went into the bathroom to freshen up. She only had thirty minutes to prepare for her meeting with Alex Liberty. Maybe *he* was the man of her dreams.

******

"What am I looking for? I'm looking for love, I suppose," Alex said a little while later, sipping a tall, dark roast coffee.

Angelique didn't know why she had asked the question. She hardly knew this man. Wasn't this getting way too personal, way too fast? But she liked where the conversation was going. And she liked Alex's appearance—she found him sexy. Trying to appear indiscreet, she sized him up as he elaborated. He had short gelled brown hair, stood about six-foot-three with a lean and muscular frame, was well-dressed in a black polo long-sleeve shirt, blue Levi jeans, black point-toe alligator shoes and a matching black belt. His brilliant blue eyes, carved nose and high cheekbones reminded her of a younger version of Dolph Lundgren. He claimed to be an advertising executive with a downtown ad agency.

"I mean, really, when it comes down to it, isn't that a fundamental human need—to be loved by a soulmate? To have that special person to come home to, confide in, rely on, trust, do things with—and return the love and affection?" Alex asked.

Angelique sighed. It was what she had been searching for all her young life. She needed to be needed. Alex was saying all the right things. He could talk the talk. She wondered if he could walk the walk. "It is what we all want. But it isn't easy to find."

"You got that right," Alex said as he ogled an attractive blonde who had just stepped in line for a coffee. The blonde noticed his approving glance and smiled.

Angelique grimaced. *Just like all men. Can't stop the wandering eyes. Undressing her with his eyes.*

Alex caught the disapproving look and flushed ever so slightly—caught red-handed. And red-faced.

Let's see him talk himself out of this one.

"The problem is," he continued. "We're all so caught up in the pursuit of material wealth that we lose sight of what really matters. We try and collect all this money so we can live better and then by the time we have enough we're way too old to enjoy it. It's a vicious cycle."

To Angelique's ears, his words had suddenly lost their profundity. She didn't even know this man, but jealousy was getting the better of her. She rolled her gaze to a well-dressed, attractive black man talking animatedly with someone a few tables away. The man smiled at her, which she promptly returned.

Two can play at that game.

Alex followed her gaze and grinned slightly. He wasn't a stupid man, Angelique thought. He knew her game.

But, in spite of what she now viewed as deficiencies, she still found Alex attractive. And she was horny as hell. Maybe a good sex session was exactly what she needed to take her mind off Matt. She had thought earlier about sending an apologetic email, asking for his forgiveness and pleading for his love.

She pushed the thought away and smiled at Alex. He returned the smile with a mouth full of perfect veneers, maybe even implants. The tooth reconstruction alone must have cost at least $20,000. He had money.

"Interesting point," Angelique said, trying on her most charming tone. She uncrossed her legs for a split-second and spotted Alex's eyes flash down and up quickly. She wasn't wearing panties. Caught again, vying for a crotch-shot. He wanted her. Of that, she was sure.

"Wouldn't the world be so much easier if all this materialism weren't a part of it? Live like Indians, off the land or something," Angelique said.

"The problem is, we're so accustomed to our creature comforts most of us couldn't handle it. But, I agree with you. I think people would play far fewer games if the need for survival was priority number one."

Some part of Angelique's mind flashed back to a simpler existence and an image formed. She was in a cornfield, surrounded by rugged mountains, playing tag with her sister—*What was her name?*—racing through the field laughing, without a care in the world. But then she heard a scream, her world went black, she felt herself being hoisted into a vehicle and hauled away. A cold chill crept up her spine when she realized who the little girl was. *What the hell was that image? Was that little girl me?*

"Are you okay?" Alex asked. "You look kind of sad. Your eyes went far away for a few seconds."

Angelique quickly regained her composure. "It's nothing. I was just thinking of a small problem at work. But I'll sort it out. Who wants to talk business now, anyway?"

"Not me, that's for sure. I get enough of it."

"I like you. Why don't we go have a drink somewhere more private and continue this discussion?"

Chapter Seven

"I think I've had enough of this discussion," Joe Andreas said. "If all you're willing to cough up is ten grand, you'll be hearing from my lawyer."

Matt had answered the phone in the coffee shop earlier in the day and told the courier he would call him back when he arrived home. On his arrival, his head had begun to throb painfully, not least of all because of the nasty email from Sal and the ugly scene at Sorento with Angelique. So he had popped three painkillers, and fallen asleep on the couch for three hours. It was now 8:30 at night. He had been on the phone with Joe for just over five minutes.

He had offered Joe $5,000 initially, and when the courier refused, claiming whiplash, he had upped the anti to $10,000. But that wasn't good enough for this clown.

Matt remembered what Sal had said. *Stall.* "Listen, can you give me some time to think about it?"

"How much time? I'm in a lot of pain here."

Matt scratched his head. *At least find out how much he wants, you numbskull.* "How much money will make you go away?"

There was a momentary silence on the line.

"I want $100,000 minimum or I'll sue you for a lot more than that."

It would be about five minutes later that Matt would realize he had said the wrong thing. He would wonder if his head was more messed up than he thought. "You're fucking crazy if you think I'm going to give you $100,000. You hit me. I went through the intersection on a green light."

"You hit me and you ran a red. You'll be hearing from my lawyer." The phone went dead. Matt grimaced, walked into the bathroom and splashed some cold water on his face.

He returned to the living room, stared at the darkening sky of the picturesque cityscape for a few minutes, noticing the clouds were finally dispersing. Maybe tomorrow would be sunny for a change. It had rained constantly for a week. He sat down on the couch and decided to check his cell phone for messages. He turned it on and it instantly started chiming—six voicemails and five text messages.

He went through the messages, half-expecting to get an apology from Sal and a pleading request from Angelique to get back together. Sal hadn't called. *Fuck him. I'm going to give him a wide berth for a while. I don't need that negative shit in my life. I've got enough.*

Angelique had not called. *What am I going to do with her? I guess it's already been done. She turns me on so much, though. And something else. Chemistry? But she's a fucking nutcase, dude. Remember that. Maybe Sal was right?*

The other messages were from his secretary Michelle. Some clients in need of investment consultations had decided to cancel their appointments instead of rescheduling. They didn't want a real estate investment consultant who wasn't available. *I say jump, you ask how high.* It was the way the Vancouver business climate operated. People wanted an answer yesterday. If you didn't deliver the right result on time, oftentimes you were punted curbside. Strong loyalties were hard to forge. Most of the loyalties were fickle at best. Clients always had their eyes open for a better deal and a faster result. Or maybe they had already discovered the black mark—Able Property Management's judgment against Matt. Word traveled fast in the real estate community. It was a small, interconnected network.

Matt's injuries—mental and physical—were costing him money at a time when he needed it most.

He had hung up a shingle five years ago in a prestigious office building in the downtown core. Other than his secretary (more like an executive assistant) who was also a licensed realtor, Matt was a one-man operation. He had tried taking on a partner, but the marriage of sorts had disintegrated two years later when he discovered Scott Sopkin was making side deals with clients and keeping all the money. Greed had gotten the better of Sopkin. So Matt had turfed his ass from Global Equity Investments and now sailed the ship alongside Michelle.

Although Matt had ten years of experience as a commercial and residential realtor, his new title, Real Estate Investment Consultant, had narrowed his focus to managing large property portfolios. He would advise clients when to buy, sell and refinance. He also laid out a blueprint that detailed how to grow wealth and retire through the acquisition and eventual disposition of rental properties. Occasionally, this blueprint called for the purchase of a flip property to renovate and resell for a profit.

Matt was well-versed in analyzing real estate properties using rate of return formulas such as Capitalization Rate, Gross Rent Multipliers and Cash-on-Cash Equity Rate of Return. With barebones financials, he could determine a property's profitability in less than five minutes. He had created many millionaires in the city. Before the real estate market tanked, his services were in high demand. Now, clients were a little more skeptical of real estate acquisition, although in Matt's mind they should be thinking the opposite. There were deals to be had and it was up to him to convince his clients of that. But, with three vacant rental properties, he was no longer practicing what he preached.

Calm waters had been replaced by stormy seas.

His outsourced team included lawyers, accountants, renovation contractors, realtors and up until recently, a property management company. Able Property Management had screwed him, to be sure. Problem was, a third of his clients also used Able, at one time on Matt's list of preferred property managers. Now he was faced with the daunting task of telling his clients he had fucked up with the Able recommendation. The ripple effect could sink an already water-logged ship. And, in a sea of shady property management companies (Matt found ninety per cent of them stole from their clients) he was tasked with the responsibility of finding another honest and competent company to fill in the missing piece of the puzzle. Matt's investment recommendations called for a hands-off approach for the investor. It had to be turn-key to sell it to his clientele.

He listened to the last message. His lawyer, Sarah Walker, wanted him to call at his earliest convenience. She had some good news, which cheered Matt a little. Maybe things would work out. Besides, he had to talk to her about that wing-nut courier anyway. That was something that couldn't wait. It was only a matter of time before a process server showed up at his door with a pizza box containing a lawsuit. Matt had seen many process server tricks—the deceptive tactic was not out of the realm of possibility.

Sarah picked up on the first ring.

"You got my message?" she asked.

"Yeah."

"I heard about your accident. Are you okay?"

"I think so."

"You think so? Have you been to the hospital?"

"No."

"Are you daft or something?" One thing about Sarah, she didn't mince words. Maybe it was a lawyer thing.

Matt brushed it off. "I'll go see my doctor tomorrow." Tell people what they want to hear and they'll leave you alone. "Tell me about the good news."

"I got the judgment overturned. You don't have a black mark on your record anymore."

Matt sighed. "What else?"

"You'll be getting the tenant security deposits returned"

Matt did a quick calculation. "What about the $7,500 they stole?"

"I don't know about that. They claim you interfered with their property management services, cost them a lot of money."

"That's bullshit."

"I know, Matt ... calm down. At least we've got the judgment overturned and your tenants will be getting what's owed to them."

"You're right. Sorry. That *is* a big relief. Thanks. Where do we go from here?"

"You tell me. You're the client."

"What's your advice?"

"We either go after them for $7,500—with punitive damages we might be able to bring that up to $20,000—or we try to settle, which means both parties sign a release saying effectively the matter has been resolved and there will be no further litigation from either side. For your part, you have to decide whether it's worth it to sue for $20,000. Guaranteed, they'll counter-sue."

Matt digested the so-called victory. He was out of pocket $7,500—likely a $15,000 legal bill—and now had three vacant properties as a result of incompetence by Able Property Management. He would like to hang Rod Badrickis by a rope and watch him choke until his eyes popped from their sockets; or put a gun to his head and blow his brains out. *Oh, right. I'm in Canada. You can't do that here. This isn't the Wild West. I forgot. How daft of me. Maybe Sarah's right. I am daft.*

"Think about it for a few days and let me know what you want to do," Sarah said.

"Okay. I'll think about it. There's something else we need to talk about."

"I was waiting for you to get to that."

Matt realized Sarah had probably already told Michelle about the courier accident. He recounted it and the follow-up conversations to the best of his recollection. He was going to omit the part where he exploded on the courier, but thought better of it at the last second. Sarah was his lawyer. If she was going to help him, she would need to know everything.

"I need to think this one through," Sarah said. "If he phones you—and chances are he'll call again before he goes to a lawyer—don't be confrontational, whatever you do. And don't swear at him. Tell him calmly that you're thinking about it and you need more time. Stall him for a few days. And don't call him until I sort this out."

Matt digested the advice. *More billable hours. Money I don't have.* But he had a longstanding and loyal relationship with Sarah. She was one of the few lawyers who didn't overbill and would give him payment terms. He promised to call her tomorrow. He knew after the call ended she would be working until at least one in the morning. It was just what Sarah did, to the exclusion of just about everything else in her life, including a relationship. She was a smart, single, attractive, hardworking woman. How could she possibly find the time to juggle a relationship while working fourteen hours a day, six days a week? Hell, she barely had time to sleep or eat, never mind love.

But love, or some powerful emotion approximating it, was exactly what entered Matt's mind three hours later when he opened the inbox to his Gmail account on his office laptop computer and discovered a message from Angelique. *Why am I getting an erection?*

It was a quarter to midnight. The message had arrived three minutes ago. He took two deep breaths and read:

> *I cannot sleep. I feel I have done something wrong. I do not want to leave you now. I feel that you live inside of me and that you are everything to me. Nobody ever wanted as I love you. I would give my whole life to make you happy. I want to love you until I die.*
>
> *Sometimes I think I was born for you. You have something special, very different from others. Have you*

ever entered into the other? It's you—you're the one for me. I want your heart. I'm happy with you. I will always be here. I will leave you never, unless you want me to leave.

I am not able to get away from you. I will always be honest, always live for you. If you knew that you make me so lacking. I like the way you are. I love you with my heart.

Please come back to me, Matt. Teach me how to behave to make you happy. You are much older than I and I don't have a lot of experience in these matters. Sometimes maybe I'm even a little immature. But, with your help, I know we can make it. Please contact me soon. I won't sleep until I hear from you. I love you with all my heart.

Many kisses and hugs. Angelique

Out of respect—and to see where the relationship would go—Matt had deleted his Plenty of Fish profile a day after meeting Angelique. He had been quick to notice she had not. Lots of lip service to the word love. But her actions were speaking much louder. To keep an eye on her, he had set up a phony account—under the alias Mike Rider—complete with a phony photo and alias email account. He quickly logged into the account, punched in Angelique's profile number and her status button flashed—*online now, if you'd like to chat.*

Fucking conniving bitch. Telling me all this bullshit, while she's surfing the net and hooking up with other guys. It hadn't been the first time he had caught Angelique online. After a rather memorable lovemaking session two weeks ago, he had checked her status about an hour after she had left his condo and discovered her online. He had caught her online at least three times after that. When he had nonchalantly questioned Angelique, she had feigned innocence: "Since I've met you, I haven't been on any dating sites." Caught in the first lie.

She loves me, she loves me not. She loves me tonight. Tomorrow she finds another guy, she loves me not.

He suspected there were more sites, but hadn't bothered checking. Each discovery would just be another disappointment, another red flag to add to the growing collection.

Fighting an urge to respond to Angelique's email—even call her—he closed his email account and googled property management companies. After his early-evening nap, at least his headache had subsided. Maybe it was just a mild concussion and he wouldn't have to go to the doctor, although he had never really planned on making good on his promise to Sarah. It had been a surreptitious diversion to change the subject. With any luck, legal matters would take precedence and Sarah would forget about following up on his health.

Then he wouldn't have to lie. Sure, he lied a certain amount in his business practice. But they were white lies. Everyone told them. Matt hated lying when the lies were serious. Eventually lies bite you right in the ass—not to mention the pain they cause the recipients. *If you don't like liars, don't tell lies; otherwise you're a hypocrite. Who are you telling that to? Yourself? Angelique?*

Chapter Eight

At five past midnight, Angelique studied her computer screen, waiting for a response from Matt. She had been waiting for twenty minutes. It seemed like an eternity. She felt empty, alone and, after the disappointing one-night stand with Alex, cheap and degraded.

After a couple of drinks at a neighborhood pub, they had returned to Angelique's apartment, where Alex did her missionary-style on the couch. Her emotional frailty, along with her obsession with Matt, obstructed any carnal pleasure she might have otherwise felt. She couldn't wait for Alex to blow his load and get the hell out of her apartment. Adding insult to injury, when he finished, grabbed his jeans and started dressing, something dropped from his pocket, clinked, and rolled along the floor. She picked it up—a gold wedding band.

Alex had mentioned over drinks he was single.

"Talk the talk, but you can't walk the fucking walk, can you?" she shouted, furious, holding up the wedding ring. "You're just like all men—a liar. And not a very good one, either. Get the hell out of here now."

Watching Alex hurriedly descend the staircase a few minutes after nine, Angelique had left him with one parting shot: "By the way, loser—lose my number."

Why doesn't Matt get back to me? What's wrong with him? She frantically grabbed her cell phone and called him. It immediately went to voicemail. Either he was on the line or had turned the phone off for the night. She remembered Matt also had a landline that he used mainly for faxing. Surfing the internet, she found it. She dialed and four rings later she was greeted by the high-pitched squealing sound of a receiving fax machine. She clenched her fists and gritted her teeth.

What should I do? What should I do? But the question found an answer immediately. Angelique quickly grabbed her long black trench coat, slipped on her shoes, pocketed her cell phone and left. Matt lived only six blocks away.

A few minutes later, walking down the dimly lit streets, she jumped suddenly as a black shadow appeared in the reflection of a boutique window. She stopped, jerking her head to the side and glancing down a dark alley. A tin can rattled in the distance from the obscurity of the alley. She shivered as goosebumps crawled up her back and along her forearms. She fought an urge to run. *What's the matter with you? It's probably a cat or a dumpster-diver searching for beer can empties.*

She hurried along in spite of her mind's reassurances.

Just as she arrived at Wall Centre, a few specks of rain began spitting from the sky. The weather man had gotten it wrong—again. A thick black bank of clouds rolled in from the Pacific Ocean. Angelique flipped up the collar of her trench coat and hurried under the building's steel awning as the raindrops increased in intensity and volume. A strong wind blew in and started swirling bits of debris into mini tornadoes.

She waited by the door for eleven minutes before a young man dressed in a jogging suit and running shoes opened the door, saw Angelique, and stopped. "Are you all right?"

"I lost my keys," Angelique said, feigning a look of frustration. "My roommate's sleeping and I can't reach her."

"What's your suite number?"

"1506."

He smiled. "We're almost next-door neighbors. I'm 1616."

"I think I've seen you before," Angelique lied, offering her most seductive smile.

"I hope I see you again," the man said, holding the door open for her.

Angelique smiled, entered, and quickly boarded the elevator while the man jogged away.

She had no intention of buzzing Matt. She wasn't about to entertain the possibility of being rejected via apartment building buzzer. If Matt was going to reject her, he would have to do it in person.

Angelique arrived and knocked on the door—three hard raps.

******

Matt stared at the digital bedside clock: 1:06 am. He bolted upright in bed. *Who the hell is that?*

Just wait, they'll go away. Outside, a thunder cloud boomed, reverberating inside the bedroom. He stared at his hands, which were shaking like a recovering alcoholic's after three days in detox.

Knock ... knock ... knock.

He got out of bed, threw on a pair of jeans and a t-shirt, and approached the door. He slowly crept up to the spyhole and peeped into it. It was illuminated pinkish-brown. Someone had a finger over it.

"Who is it?" Matt asked.

"Matt, open the door. I need to see you." It was Angelique's pleading voice.

He felt blood flowing to his member. "What are you doing here? It's one o'clock in the morning."

"Open the door."

"I thought you dumped me?"

"Can we talk about this? I don't want to talk on the other side of the door."

Matt opened the door. Angelique's forlorn eyes stared at him—into him. "I'm sorry."

He led her into the living room and she sat down on the couch. He picked an armchair. "You can't come over here in the middle of the night like this."

"Did you get my email?"

He nodded.

"I meant every word of it. I love you. Can we try this over, start from the beginning?"

"Do you know what we call this in Canada—what you're doing?"

Angelique's wounded eyes met Matt's narrowing ones. She frowned.

"It's called stalking—and it's a criminal offence." Matt felt his face flush with anger, mixed with another emotion—fear. Six years ago, he had dated an Asian woman for a week, slept with her twice, and decided they weren't on the same wavelength. Perhaps he should have told Margaret Chong as much, but after such a short amount of time he felt he didn't owe her an explanation. It wasn't like they had a committed relationship. So he had just stopped returning her calls.

But it didn't take long for Margaret to start stalking Matt. Following him down the street on foot, pursuing him in her vehicle, showing up at his then-basement suite and banging on the windows in the middle of the night; even showing up at his office and invading client meetings. Matt was sure few people realized the horror of being stalked, unless they had actually experienced it; the worry, fear and wondering when the mentally imbalanced person might decide to take things a step further and resort to violence or murder. Eventually the police became involved and he got a restraining order. But that didn't stop Margaret.

But fortunately, what did stop her was a deportation order from Canadian immigration officials. Authorities had learned Margaret was suspected in the murders of at least three men she had dated in Hong Kong. She was later convicted on all counts. He had been lucky to have escaped with his life. *Goodbye and good riddance, Margaret.*

The entire traumatic ordeal flashed through Matt's mind like a lightning bolt as thunder boomed and reverberated through the room. He looked at Angelique, wondering if she was capable of murder. *Everyone's capable of murder. You just have to push the right triggers. Be careful.*

Angelique twisted in her seat. "I'm not a stalker. I'm Mexican. We're hot-blooded and passionate. If it's a weakness to be passionate, then I have it. If it's a weakness to fall in love quickly, then yes, I have it. And yes, I anger quickly. But I also calm down and forget quickly. It's only because I love you. When I don't hear from you, it frustrates me. I want to know where you are."

"What kind of love is that, Angelique? It sounds more like an obsession. That's your insecurity, if you want to know where I am at every waking moment, and you're calling all the time, texting, emailing, expecting an immediate response. I can't have a relationship like that. I've got enough shit in my life right now to have to worry that if I don't get back to you within a few minutes, you'll fly off the handle and start sending nasty emails, wondering and worrying where I am—maybe thinking I'm with another woman or something." *Careful what you say.*

Angelique's eyes narrowed. "Have you been with another woman?"

Matt looked surprised. "You only dumped me a little while ago. And I've got a concussion, for fuck sakes. No, I haven't." He was about to ask her the same question, but bit his tongue. *Don't push the envelope. You have no idea what you're dealing with.*

"Can I explain something to you?" Angelique asked.

"By all means."

"I'm a little crazy and extreme when I like someone. I just want to talk, and talk and talk. Be with them all the time. No one's ever made me feel like you do. Sometimes I feel like a little girl about to go to school for the first time—all the fear that goes along with it. And I get so afraid I want to push you away before you can hurt me. That's what happened earlier today. I realized it soon after it happened. Help me change. I'm young, but I'm an adult and I know what I want. And it's you."

The info dump was overloading Matt's compromised senses. At the same time, he didn't want an explosive scene right now with a woman who had just admitted to being extreme and crazy. *Get rid of her. But do it nicely.*

"Just remember a few things," Angelique said. "You also told me you love me—more than once. Sure, it might have been online, but I'm not a computer plug-in. I'm a human being, flesh and blood."

Matt frowned. He had said he loved her. Did he mean it, did he feel it at the time he said it? One part of him thought he had. Another part of him wanted to get as far away from this mentally imbalanced woman as possible. He was confused again, not least of all because a dull throbbing pain had resurfaced in his head.

Thunder boomed, lightning flashed over the city skyline, and the rain turned torrential in an instant.

Matt stood up and walked to the window, staring at the lightning flashes.

Angelique stood up and approached.

Matt jumped as she touched his arm.

"Don't be afraid of me," she said. "I want to be your painting in motion. My life has no meaning without you. I just want to feel needed, useful."

Matt gazed into sad eyes and felt a moment of tenderness. "I'll think about it, okay?"

Angelique moved closer and ran the back of her hand along Matt's stubble. She nodded. "Don't think about it too long. I can take love away as quickly as I can give it. Sure, I suffer. But I can do it. And you're responsible for this feeling. It's your fault I fell in love with you."

There was some flash in her dark eyes that suggested she was playing him, at least on the last line. But Matt was not familiar enough with her sense of humor to get it, even if it was intended as some kind of an ironic joke.

Suddenly, she hugged him tightly. He returned the embrace, slowly gliding his stubbly cheek across her face. He pulled away slightly, staring into her eyes. She smiled and kissed him. It turned into a long, passionate kiss. *God, she turns me on.*

Is that the male shallow way of thinking—purely physical? I must be crazy, too.

Matt stepped back. "Can we talk about this tomorrow? I've got a pounding headache. It's late and I have a lot of work tomorrow."

She stepped away. "Thanks for listening to me. I want everything with you."

Matt nodded. He couldn't help the tingly feelings permeating his body. "It's ugly out there. I'll call you a cab."

******

Angelique didn't recognize the phone number on her cell phone twenty minutes later as she climbed stairs to her apartment. "Hello?"

"Angelique Augusto?"

"It's me."

"This is Detective Ben Lyons from the Vancouver Homicide Squad. Sorry to bother you so late. Do you know an Alex Liberty?"

A long pause.

"I just met him briefly, why?"

"He was slashed to pieces a few hours ago—his body was dropped in a dumpster a short distance from your apartment. We found your business card in his pocket. I think we need to talk."

Chapter Nine

Jesus didn't want to talk, even though he had been asked a question. He had just been convicted of second-degree murder and sentenced to eight years in prison. He had said enough during the short trial. The judge, while sympathetic to Jesus's need to preserve his honor and dignity, meted out the minimum sentence required of him by law. There was no question about the evidence. There had been at least twenty witnesses to the killing.

Jesus's lawyer, Victor Sanchez, the court-appointed Ombudsman (few accused locals could afford to hire a lawyer) had argued self-defense. But it had seemed to Jesus merely a token gesture at mitigating the sentence. Victor had told Jesus in no uncertain terms prior to entering the small courthouse that "if the judge doesn't like your face—or if you say something stupid or disrespectful—you could get twenty-five years."

Jesus wasn't even sure he should open his mouth, but Victor had encouraged it. Jesus had told of his crime serenely and proudly, convinced he had done the right thing.

Jesus wasn't unlike many inmates in the Guadalupe y Calvo prison, a mixture of Tarahumara Indians, Tepehuan Indians and Mestizo Serranos (mixed descent Native American Indians). Instead of feeling degraded, they often viewed their crimes as a badge of honor and a necessity.

Perhaps author and professor Carlos Mario Alvarado Licon (*The Sierra Tarahumara, A Wounded Land, The Culture of Violence in the Drug-Producing Zones*) explains it best:

In the Sierra homicide is no dishonor. Killing is a part of life, a circumstantial action, generally vengeance for another killing. However, on occasion, it is a symbol of pride, when vengeance was done and the law taken into one's own hands ... Homicide is a form of maintaining the social order where the official authority is absent, unjust or corrupt, and particularly where it fails to punish aggression or offense to the family.

Victor eyed Jesus and flicked an ash into an overstuffed ashtray. His tiny office was located down the hall from the courtroom. Faint sobbing echoed outside the door, a family crying about the murder conviction of one of their own.

Victor's desk was stacked high with files, papers and assorted weapons—knives, swords, handguns, machine guns, even a bloodstained baseball bat. The portly man patted down his short, greasy hair, exhaled a cloud of smoke into the tiny office and repeated his question: "Do you feel responsible for what you did?"

"I gave my story in the courtroom," Jesus said, barely able to see Victor through the stack of desk clutter and blue-gray haze of cigarette smoke.

"I know you did. But I'm doing research. I need to get it again."

Jesus sighed. *Better just get it over with.* "No, I was only defending myself."

"Is your sentence just?"

"No. It was between the two of us. The courts shouldn't get involved."

"Are you afraid to return to your home when you're released from prison?"

"No, I don't have any enemies. I didn't and don't have problems with homicide."

"Would this reaction to kill your enemies be typical of the Tarahumara principles?"

Jesus paused at that question. He knew the current drug culture had increased the murder rate among his people. It was drugs that provided the money for guns, marijuana, cocaine and alcohol. "The Tarahumara are inherently a peaceful people. We want cultural stability, rather than change. We don't initiate conflict. And typically we retreat, rather than retaliate. It's the culture of drugs that changed all that."

"How so?"

"It's obvious, isn't it?"

Victor took a long drag on his cigarette and blew a cloud of smoke into Jesus's face. "I would like you to elaborate, please."

Jesus waved a hand in front of his face. "When you have drugs, guns and money, people get paranoid and aggressive. They kill without thinking. There are entire communities that have been killed off because of feuds."

"I'm aware of most of these battles," Victor said matter-of-factly. "So, what you're telling me is it's the new order, the new law of the land, so to speak."

Jesus nodded. "It's been that way for as long as I can remember. It's all I know."

"You've never been told anything different about your people?"

"My grandfather, when I was a small boy, told me stories of a peaceful and harmonious existence, before the drug lords.

Back then we believed in a simple law called the attitude of humble silence."

"What's that?"

"It's love, humility, hope and joy."

"But you've never lived it?"

Jesus shook his head. "This is my life. Kill or be killed. My father taught me that. If I didn't kill Rodriguez, he would have killed me. Of that, I'm sure. I needed to send that message. And I'm not ashamed. I'm proud of what I've done."

"You're proud to be judge, jury and executioner?"

Jesus nodded. "I didn't make the rules. But that's what they are."

"So you don't feel like a criminal?"

"I'm not a criminal. Rodriguez is the criminal. He attacked me. He came looking for death."

"Came looking for death?"

"He threatened my livelihood, and later tried to beat me to death. He knew the consequences of his actions, but did it anyway. Once he transgressed the laws of moral human behavior, he lost all his rights as a human being—lost his right to live."

"So you're not responsible for his death?"

"I think we're going in circles. No. He's responsible. I only defended my honor, my livelihood and my life. I would do it again without hesitation."

There was a knock on the door.

"Who is it?" Victor said impatiently, grabbing a handgun on the desk. He cocked the hammer and pointed it at the door.

A voice from the other side: "I want to see my son."

Word of the conviction had spread throughout Mexico quickly. In closely-knit communities, the gossip grapevine travelled faster than the internet. Jesus's mother Esperanza, his father Audiel, and Gloria stood outside the door. They had come to say goodbye.

Victor's nervousness evaporated slowly. He laid the weapon on the desk, rose and approached the door. Before opening it, he turned to Jesus. "Thanks for that. We'll continue later."

Jesus nodded and stood, ankle and leg shackles rattling metallically.

Victor opened the door and an armed guard escorted the three inside the office.

Victor told the guard to watch the prisoner and disappeared down the hall in search of a cup of coffee.

Jesus hugged and kissed Gloria, then hugged his mother and father, while the guard produced a white cloth and began polishing his AK-47, indifferent to the family reunion.

Gloria stepped back, wiping an eye, watching sadly as Esperanza asked questions. Jesus's mother wore a colorful smock, had shoulder-length black hair, dark skin and black eyes. There was no mistaking her pure Tarahumara Indian blood. A stoic expression countenanced her worn features.

She asked Jesus questions about the sentence term, the details of the incident, and about his health. He dutifully answered.

Audiel stepped forward. He had shortly-cropped back hair and a neatly-trimmed beard. His large hands were dirty and calloused. He wore dirt-stained, torn jeans and a white, soil-stained t-shirt. He smiled broadly, exposing a mouth with missing front teeth. "I'm proud of you son. You defended the family honor."

"Thanks, Dad."

"We'll visit regularly—even if it means getting fired from my job."

"I'm not returning to Chihuahua City," Esperanza said. "I'll find something to make money here. My son needs me." She hugged Jesus again. A lone tear rolled down her cheek; she ignored it.

Gloria pulled out a tissue and began wiping her eyes.

The door swung open. Victor stood with a coffee in one hand, the other holding the arm of a shackled prisoner, two middle-aged weeping women behind him.

It was a procession of processing criminals, questions and tears. A shriek echoed from down the hall, followed by wracking sobs.

Victor regarded the people in his office. "This reunion is over. You'll have time to visit him in prison. But not today. I've got work to do."

He ushered them into the hallway. Jesus was led away by the armed guard, watched by his mother, father and Gloria. His parents stood stoic, with little expression. Gloria broke down in tears, hugged Esperanza and buried her face in the woman's bosom. Before Jesus disappeared around the corridor, Gloria said: "I'll love you until I die."

Chapter Ten

Maybe she does really love me? Maybe it's more than an obsession? Matt had finally arrived at his office and sat staring at an email, entitled *To My Love*, that had just arrived from Angelique. It was one in the afternoon and he had not yet contacted her about resuming their relationship, whatever it had been. He had mixed emotions about the whole thing. But now, reading the email, he wondered. *If someone tells you they love you enough times, don't you just start to believe it and become attracted to them, regardless of your worst fears? Wasn't love like that—a cruel and crazy emotion that makes you silly and vulnerable?*

It was a long email:

> *Dear love,*
>
> *I know yesterday I behaved badly, coming to your apartment and disturbing you. Sorry. I just went crazy and had to see you. I hope you still want to be with me. I hope you still love me because I still love you. But sometimes I feel that you won't love me enough and sometimes I decide I want to sit and not feel anything for you. This is hard ... I think I'm your girlfriend, but it's strange that sometimes this feeling seems to lie. Yet every night I sleep and dream of you.*
>
> *Each day that passes I miss you more and now I can only show my love through a message, but it will never*

be the same. If I was with you again I would take you in my hands and fill you with kisses.

Today I saw an article that spoke of love formed online. It says these romances are often stronger and I think this is my case, as I feel deep inside my heart. I hope you have not been with other women. I love you, I love you, I love you, I love you, I love you, I love you and I want you as my boyfriend, husband and to live with you forever.

I know, my love, that sometimes I lose patience. But I have so many wishes to share everything and more. I always want to hear from you, I always want more of you. Sometimes I am not content when you just send me a message with a couple of words. Sometimes your short responses scare me and I think you do not love me even half of what I love you. I have wanted so much to love you.

My love, you do not know how much I miss you! I always want to talk to you, always miss you and always want to be by your side, but that just makes you even more surprised.

Every day you're on my mind. I cannot remove from my mind what is in my heart. I keep thinking of you, imagining what you're doing at every moment, and wondering when I'll see you again.

I'm so happy I've found you. If there is such a thing as a soulmate, I believe you're mine. I want to be what you want because for me you are what I want.

Hope you're not mad at me, I hope you understand and forgive me. I hope you still want my love and affection. In my heart and mind I still want to be yours. I still want to be your love.

Please be with me again. I'll love you until I die.

Many kisses and hugs, Angelique

Finishing it, Matt couldn't help the tent growing in his black cotton slacks, nor the tingly feeling that pervaded his extremities. *Honestly, how could any man say no to that kind of passion?*

Matt had never received such passionately powerful words ever before in his life. And the words were indeed having an effect. He was about to start typing and then decided, fuck email. He wanted to talk to Angelique, tell her how much he wanted her back and couldn't wait to see her.

He dialed her number. The phone went to voicemail immediately. Either it was turned off, or she was on the other line. *With another man?* Now it was Matt doing the panicking. He hung up without leaving a message. How quickly the emotional pendulum of love swings to the other side. *Maybe I should just show up at her office? Don't be stupid. You've got appointments. Call back and leave a message. No, send an email. No, call and leave a message.* He picked up the phone and dialed.

Voicemail again. He was about to leave a message telling her he wanted her back—and to call him right away, something like that—when he noticed another email from Sal.

He hung up the phone and grimaced while reading it:

You will have to excuse my bluntness, but I have heard so many stories of men believing young poor women they've met on the internet are in love with them I almost choke—can't take any such stories anymore. I will self-destruct. I usually smile and say yes, maybe you're right. Even people with lots of experience still make those mistakes (I am not referring to you). They think young, beautiful women want them for their great personalities. New Year's resolution—I'm going to be honest (and prepared to run) next time I hear these stories. Or I will just run so I don't have to listen to it—self-destruction is no solution either. Man, do I need a vacation.

Matt frowned after reading the email. He knew Sal was under a lot of stress and badly needed some time off work. He had been putting in fourteen-hour shifts seven days a week for the last eight months. *Is that all people do in Canada—work?* It wasn't a question of if, but *when* Sal would crash and burn.

The email was the closest thing to an apology Matt would get. And Sal didn't know what the fuck he was talking about with respect to Angelique's feelings for Matt. But Sal was his friend—for better or worse. It was an axiom of friendship—sometimes you hate them, other times you love them. He made a mental note to call Sal later in the day.

First, there was another call he had to make. He picked up the phone again, determined to leave a message if he got Angelique's voicemail again.

There was a knock on his office door.

Michelle's voice: "Are you decent?"

Matt put down the phone. "Come in."

She opened the door, a pizza box in one hand. A man wearing a Pizza Hut delivery outfit stood behind her. "This is a surprise," Michelle said. "You ordered pizza for lunch?"

The mock-delivery man snatched the box from Michelle's hands abruptly, entered the office, plopped it on Matt's desk and flipped open the lid. "You've just been served, Mr. Green. I hope you like Hawaiian. How many process servers provide free pizza?" He lifted the documents from the sticky cheese topping and plopped them on the desk.

The man examined the documents. "A little cheese on the bottom, but it's still a lawsuit from a Mr. Andreas for half a million. I hope your business is going well."

He turned and left.

Michelle's pale skin flushed red, one of the few times Matt had seen her blush. "Sorry."

"It's not your fault. I wouldn't have dodged it, anyway. I half-expected it."

"We may as well eat it," Michelle said, sitting down and taking a slice.

Matt realized he was hungry, so he grabbed a piece and started munching on it.

Between bites, Michelle looked at him seriously. "Do you remember Julie Macklebie?"

Matt nodded. Julie had learned of Matt's expertise with foreclosures by reading one of his website blog posts and had called him out of the blue, urging him to list her home as soon as possible. He had evaluated the dilapidated bungalow a week ago. Many of the rooms were stuffed floor-to-ceiling with junk, and the bank was about to foreclose. Julie lived with two teen-age sons, two dogs, her mother and elderly grandfather.

Julie wiped away tears as she had told Matt her story. Her ex-husband, Leonard—who she had a restraining order against—was being investigated by police in the recent murder of Julie's grandfather, Fred.

Fred had been found dead in his car in a casino parking lot, six stab wounds to the chest, slumped over in a pool of his own blood. Leonard had refinanced the property—allegedly fraudulently—just prior to the divorce, pulling out maximum equity and blowing the money before Julie's divorce lawyer had the title transferred to her name. Julie now had a house with very little equity.

Allegedly, Leonard had added Fred's name to the refinance application without his knowledge. Fred had become angry with Leonard after learning of this, and threatened to report him to police.

If that wasn't enough, Julie walked with a limp, the result of Leonard running her over with a pickup truck a few months prior to the divorce. The incident had nearly killed her, had deprived her of her livelihood, and left her permanently handicapped. The only reason she had not reported the attempted murder to police, she said, was because, "I don't want to deprive my kids of a father."

But now, due to recent events, Leonard was being investigated by police for mortgage fraud, attempted murder and first-degree murder of Julie's grandfather. Out of fear for his life, Matt had refused to list the property. But he never forgot the pleading look in Julie's sad eyes as he left her house that afternoon. Probably would never forget it.

"What about her?" Matt said, putting down the pizza slice. A chunk got stuck in his throat and he coughed, before reaching for a glass of water and washing it down.

"Are you okay?" Michelle asked.

He nodded as the color drained from his face. He probably would never forget the fear he had felt leaving that residence either.

"Anyway, Julie called today. She pleaded for you to take the listing. She was crying and everything. I didn't have the heart to say no over the phone. I told her I'd ask you again."

"Sorry. I'm not touching it. I don't want that psycho ex hunting me down. Forget it. Tell her to find another realtor."

"She says no one else will go near it."

"I'm not surprised." Matt stared at the half-eaten pizza slice. He had lost his appetite.

A door opened outside Matt's office and both heads turned. Michelle stood up. "I think that's your one-thirty."

"Is it Marilyn Stewart?" She was an impatient investor who had threatened to take her business elsewhere if Matt wouldn't meet with her on her schedule.

You say jump, I ask how high? Matt wished he had enough money to tell her to fuck off.

Michelle nodded and gave him that look. Make haste.

"Tell her I'll be right out."

Michelle paused. "She doesn't like to wait."

Matt waved her out the door. "I'll be less than five minutes."

Michelle left and Matt dialed Angelique, after call-forwarding his cell to the office line. This time he did leave a message: "Honey, I got your email and I was blown away. No one's ever written me such powerful words of passion. I want you back. I love you. Call when you have a chance."

He hung up. *I've said it. I've said the L-word. Did I mean it? It feels real, so I must have meant it. Or is the little head doing the thinking again?* Matt didn't know. But he knew—regardless of the outcome—he was jumping on the rollercoaster with Angelique to discover first-hand if it would be a crash-and-burn landing or the rollercoaster would fly off into the sunset and land smoothly in some idyllic and pastoral rural setting, where the two would live happily ever after. Maybe with a few bumps along the way, but bumps were inevitable. *Depends on how you handle them.*

He ran a hand along a clean-shaven face. *Does it matter, really, how it ends? In the whole scheme of things, does it really matter? Good or bad, it'll be a learning experience.*

His desk phone beeped and Michelle's melodious voice echoed through the speaker, jarring him out of the reverie. "Sarah is on line one. Says it's urgent." Then in a hushed tone: "Marilyn is getting impatient. I'd make it quick if I were you."

Matt picked up the phone and clicked the line. "Hi, Sarah."

"How are you feeling?" Sarah's tone was cheerful, belying the grim news she was about to deliver. She didn't wait for an answer. "Rod Badrickis's lawyer has filed another lawsuit in civil court for $100,000 in damages. Claims you obstructed the duties of Able Property Management and threatened one of his property managers with harassing calls so bad he had to quit for mental health reasons."

"That's bullshit," Matt said, but then some vague memories floated into a head that still ached dully. He remembered making at least three calls that could possibly be construed as threatening. To make matters worse, he couldn't remember the content of the third call. He had been so worried about his dwindling finances as a result of Able's incompetence, he had committed the cardinal sin—drunk-dialing property manager Rick Folly at ten at night. He knew he'd said something like, "Make the problem go away or you'll be hearing from me again." Or was it, "Get your shit together or there'll be hell to pay."

Could that be considered harassment? Probably. Could it be considered a threat? Probably. Had Able taped the conversations? In all likelihood, yes. Had they taken the tapes to the police? Good possibility.

"Have you told me everything?" Sarah asked.

"I did make some calls. I was upset."

"Matt, how many times do I have to tell you? Threats don't work in a lawful world."

"Can we talk about this later? I have a meeting."

"Call me when you're done."

"Before I go, you should know that courier is suing me."

"Michelle already told me. She's sending me the paperwork. And just so you know, Able could also charge you with harassment and uttering death threats in a criminal court, in addition to the civil case they just filed."

Matt sighed. "We'll talk later." He hung up.

He went into the reception area and noticed Marilyn had left. "What happened?" he asked Michelle, who was busy at her desk.

She looked up from a file. "Sorry, she stormed out."

"Stormed out?" Matt checked the time. "It's one-thirty-five. She couldn't wait five minutes?"

"Guess not. I tried to make her wait ... I said I'd get you right away, but she wouldn't listen. Said she didn't like the vibe here anymore ... something about Able Property Management. Wants to take her business elsewhere."

Matt thought about it. Three of Marilyn's properties were managed by Able. It had been his recommendation. Had Rod Badrickis started badmouthing Matt already, trashing the credibility of his company? He thought so. He made a mental note to call Marilyn later in the day, kiss her rotund ass, and try to salvage the account, even though it meant admitting he had fucked up with his selection of Able.

Matt extracted a sheet of paper from his pocket and handed it to Michelle.

"What's this?"

"It's a list of property management companies. Could you check them out and try to get a read on which one might do business with a modicum of honesty and competency?"

She took the paper. "Sure ... are you okay? You look white."

Matt nodded unconvincingly. He explained the news about Able, although he felt certain Michelle already knew. It didn't matter. Michelle was loyal to a fault, part of his team, part of his small inner circle, one of the very few people he could fully trust. He finished the update. "I see you filled Sarah in on the courier lawsuit?"

She nodded.

"The paperwork's in my office. Help yourself to it. When's my next appointment?"

"Four o'clock."

"Who is it?"

"Rod Vermooth. Saw your blog on foreclosures and says he wants to do some flippers."

Matt nodded. Most of the people who contacted him about foreclosures were under the misconception you could buy one with no money down. Half the time, they weren't gainfully employed and couldn't even get mortgage financing. For the ones who could get financing, half the time they didn't know a thing about renovations. When you actually crunched the numbers, about one in twenty actually had half a brain, could obtain financing or had cash, and could make money with flippers. It was a numbers game. But you had to work the numbers if you wanted to make money.

He had initially met Marilyn through his foreclosure blogs. Under Matt's tutelage, two years later she had acquired $1.6 million in real estate equity. But Marilyn's loyalty to her business advisor was akin to the loyalty a prostitute has to a trick.

Rod Vermooth? What the hell kind of name is that? "What's your read on him?" Matt asked.

"Sounds like he can get a mortgage. Works as a manager at Shopper's Drug Mart. Ten-year history. Says he's good with tools. He comes across as pretty smooth. I don't know. You'll know when you meet him. You always do."

At one time Matt would have believed that. Now, he wasn't so sure how good his gut instincts were. Seems they had been lying to him lately. "I'm going to get some fresh air. Do you want me to bring anything back?"

Michelle smiled a winning smile that would disarm even the stodgiest man. "I've got pizza, remember? But thanks. Do you want me to take your calls?"

"No. But let me know if there's anything urgent. Otherwise, please don't bother me."

Michelle nodded. "Enjoy your walk. Looks like the sun is finally poking out."

Matt left his Georgia Street office building and hailed a cab. His Supra was parked a few blocks away at his apartment, but he didn't want to drive. He planned on going to Locarno Beach, near the University of British Columbia, where it was quiet and secluded. He wanted to sit and think, undisturbed by people.

But his phone rang just as a taxi pulled up. He held out an index finger to the driver while he took the call from Angelique.

She was sobbing.

"What's wrong?" he asked.

"I just got home from a police interrogation. They think I ... I killed someone."

"Do you want me to come over?"

"Please ... I need you right now."

Matt climbed into the taxi and gave Angelique's address to the driver. A few minutes later, Angelique buzzed him in and he ascended the stairs to her apartment. She stood in the hallway in a black mid-length dress, wiping teary eyes with a tissue. Her long hair was in disarray.

"Come here," she said. "I got your message. Thanks for taking me back. I'm crazy about you."

They embraced warmly. Matt kissed Angelique and felt the familiar stirrings of desire that usually accompanied any and all contact with her.

"What happened?" Matt asked as they sat side-by-side on a sofa. A small part of his brain wondered if Angelique was capable of murder. *Everyone is, remember?*

Angelique's eyes were puffy and bloodshot. She looked like she hadn't slept. Her eyes darted nervously around the apartment as she spoke, as if a hidden predator was stalking her, waiting for the perfect moment to strike.

She explained about the phone call from Detective Lyons and the subsequent interrogation at the police station. "I told him it wasn't me. I didn't kill Alex Liberty. I didn't kill him. You have to believe me. You of all people have to believe me."

"I believe you," Matt said, unsure if it was true. "So what's the upshot? Are they charging you with murder?"

"Not yet. But Ben Lyons said something that suggests I haven't been ruled out as a suspect."

"What might that have been?"

"'Whatever you do, don't leave town.'"

Matt thought about it. Caught up in the emotion of the day, there was something he was forgetting to ask. Then it hit him like a sledgehammer. Angelique had cleverly omitted some important details.

"What makes the police suspect you? Do you know this guy, Liberty?" Matt wasn't sure he was prepared to hear the answer.

Angelique rose from the couch and paused, staring at Matt earnestly. "Do you want something to drink? How about a glass of red wine?"

Matt thought he might need the sedating effects of alcohol for what he was about to hear. "Sure."

Angelique went into the kitchen and returned with two glasses of wine, handing one to Matt and sitting in an armchair.

"Should we toast?" Matt asked sarcastically.

She ignored the question. Her expression grew dark. "I'm going to tell you everything. This isn't easy for me, because I love you so much."

Matt felt a lump of pain rising in his throat. He took a long drink of wine, hoping to push the lump back into the pit of his stomach.

"I met Alex in the Starbucks just up the road. I didn't do anything with him until last night, after I broke it off with you. I would never fool around on you. I'll be honest, I've fooled around before on boyfriends, but you're different. I would not sleep around on you."

Matt stayed silent and took another gulp of wine. She was in a lot of trouble. This was not the time or place for jealously, although he felt a small dose of the useless emotion coursing through his veins. Maybe it was just the wine?

Angelique set her glass on the coffee table without taking a sip and continued: "I hate to say this ... but I brought him up to my apartment and slept with him. Afterward, I found out he was married and kicked him out. A few hours later I started feeling guilty as hell and went to your apartment. I'm so sorry."

Shit, Matt thought, ignoring his hurt feelings. He tried to rationalize them. In their short time dating, had they promised monogamous commitments to one another? Matt didn't think so. But he wondered, now that they were getting serious, if that's what they were getting, was Angelique still surfing the web, looking for men? Was she still connected? It would be easy to check. He had the alias account, after all.

But what slowly became more worrisome was the thought that he also might be implicated in the murder. According to Angelique's account, she had been at Matt's apartment some time during or after Liberty had been murdered. Surely the detective had already questioned her on her whereabouts during the murder. Surely she had told him. The homicide detective probably already thought Matt may have been an accomplice to or a co-perpetrator of murder.

"So you told the detective you came to my apartment that night?"

Angelique frowned and nodded.

"Where did you tell him you were before that?"

"I told him I kicked Liberty out at nine at night. That I went to your place at about one in the morning."

"He's going to want to talk to me."

Angelique picked up a business card from the coffee table and handed it to Matt. "He wants you to call him."

Matt set the card on the table and thought. Finally, he said: "Did he read you your rights?"

"Not yet."

"I think you need a lawyer."

"I didn't do anything."

"It doesn't matter. This isn't the Wild West. Your alibi isn't airtight, it looks like you have motive and there's probably a lot of circumstantial evidence. Do you know a good lawyer?"

Angelique shook her head and finally took a sip of wine.

Matt knew he had at least two lawyers to call prior to his four o'clock. He needed some legal advice before he talked to this Detective Lyons. He didn't trust the police. He had heard far too many stories of innocent people being wrongly convicted of murder. "I'm going to get us a lawyer."

"I don't have money for that. And I hate going into debt—hate borrowing money from people."

"We don't have a choice. This is serious shit. Don't worry, we'll work something out." Matt finished his wine and stood up. "Don't talk to that detective until you hear from me. Don't answer his calls; don't let him in your door. You got that?"

Angelique nodded.

"You promise?"

"I swear."

"I should go." Matt approached the door. He opened it, expecting Angelique to accompany him for a goodbye kiss.

He would get more than he bargained for.

Angelique rose and stood in the middle of the living room. She pulled the top of her black dress down, exposing those perfectly-shaped, voluptuous size 44-DD breasts. She wasn't wearing a bra. So big, yet they defied gravity. Her coffee-brown aureoles were the size of peaches. Erect nipples—like thimbles—jutted out about an inch. She grinned, massaging her left nipple with one hand. "Are you sure you can't stay for a while? Don't you want some of these?"

Matt glanced at his smart phone: 2:43 pm. He couldn't wipe the grin off his face if he wanted to, nor could he stop the little pirate captain from commanding the ship through potentially stormy seas—the sail was at full mast.

He closed the door quickly, took four steps, grasping the shapely objects of his desire with both hands. Soon, he was licking, kissing, caressing those beautiful melons.

Angelique moaned softly, gently lifted a hand and escorted him into the bedroom.

For the time being, the time for talk was over.

Chapter Eleven

"Don't talk so much." It was a Tepehuan Indian scolding a mestizo inmate in a small cell Jesus shared with four other prisoners, all incarcerated for murder convictions.

"What did you say?" the mestizo asked.

Jesus had listened to the discussion for the last half hour. He sensed things were about to turn ugly.

The muscular mestizo had been bragging about how he had stabbed his wife to death after learning of her infidelity. "It's the only thing you can do," he had said, although he admitted to having three mistresses. "Normally the police don't do anything at all if you kill your wife. They would do the same thing, so they don't look at it as that serious. Besides, there's no money in it for them usually, so what do they care?"

The hard-faced Tepehuan had listened impassively until the mestizo had moved on to bragging about some of his other kills. "I'm a hundred per cent killer," he said, glowering at the Tepehuan. "My family once got into a dispute with some Tepehuan neighbors. I lost two brothers, a cousin and a sister, but the whole Tepehuan family was murdered—fifteen people, most of them killed at my hands." He delivered the last line while narrowing his eyes and scowling at the indigenous Tepehuan, who sat cross-legged, barely making eye contact.

In another corner, two Tarahumara men sat cross-legged, occasionally glancing disinterestedly at the mestizo, who paced back and forth, waving his arms while educating his fellow inmates on his talent for killing.

Jesus sat off by himself in a far corner of the dungeon-like cell.

The mestizo narrowed his black eyes at the Tepehuan and repeated the question: "What did you say? You tell me not to talk so much?"

The Tepehuan brought his gaze to the cracked, damp concrete floor.

The two Tarahumara Indians stared impassively while Jesus observed from a distance.

Shafts of sunlight shone through a small overhead steel-barred window. Dogs barked outside. Chickens clucked. The joyful shouts of children playing echoed in the small chamber, along with the steady din of vehicular traffic.

The mestizo now stood in front of the Tepehuan. He removed a well-worn cowboy hat and kneeled down, inching a scarred and stubbly face closer to the man who would dare to question his monologue on murder. "What's your name?"

The Tepuhuan made eye contact, glowering. "They call me Matalo. I don't have to tell you that means kill him."

"Matalo," the mestizo said. "You couldn't kill a horse-fly off the ass of a mule. And, for your information, my name is Isidrio Garza. Have you heard of me before?"

Matalo had heard the name. Isidrio was infamous in the region as a fearless and brutal killer of many men. He was a killer-for-hire with cartel connections. He also killed to settle a score or merely to "stay sharp," as he liked to put it.

Now he had a score to settle. He brought his face closer to Matalo's.

Matalo spit in Isidrio's face defiantly. Before Isidrio could retaliate, Matalo leaped to his feet head-butted him. Their foreheads cracked together and Isidrio reeled back, swiping a small cut above his eyebrow that dribbled blood.

In an instant, Matalo attacked.

He had to mete out justice. His honor had been besmirched, not to mention the honor of his family. Two years ago, Isidrio had put a bullet through Matalo's grandmother's head over a disagreement on the price of cocaine she had sold him. Matalo's mother had urged him to avenge that crime. The only thing that stopped him was the knowledge it would spell the death of most—if not all—of his remaining family members. His mother had never forgiven him.

Also, Matalo would rather die than look like a coward in front of others. The indigenous tribes didn't always play nice together. They had a history of violence and bloodshed.

Mounting Isidrio, Matalo hammered him in the face with large, calloused, dirty fists. Three shots—*wack wack wack*—before Isidrio bucked and bounced the smaller Indian into the air. As Matalo hit the dirt and rolled, Isidrio leaped to his feet and delivered a hard kick to the side of Matalo's head—*thwack*.

Blood sprayed from Matalo's mouth. A tooth flew and rolled to a stop in front of a Tarahumara sitting cross-legged, watching the action stone-faced, as if he was watching a soap opera on television. He glanced at the tooth with minor annoyance and slowly returned his gaze to the life-and-death battle.

Isidro delivered another kick—*thwack*—and Matalo rolled closer to the concrete wall. Isidrio thrust his leg forward again to deliver another blow and Matalo quickly swept an arm out, grabbed the cowboy-booted foot and jerked it upward.

Isidrio crashed to the ground with a thud and an expletive: "Fucking son of a bitch ... your mother's a fucking whore."

Dazed, Matalo crawled on top of the fallen man. He clawed at Isidrio's eyes, raking a five-finger trail of blood down his face.

Isidrio bucked, but Matalo raked with the other hand, sprouting little red rivers.

Isidrio bucked again, twisting his large frame at the same time, and rolled Matalo off.

The Tarahumara men watched, motionless and silent. This was not their fight. Jesus went to stand but an elder Tarahumara scowled and he quickly sat down.

Isidrio sprang to his feet and repeatedly kicked Matalo in the head, mouth, nose, eyes and face—*thwack thwack thwack thwack thwack thwack thwack thwack thwack.*

Jesus put his hands to his face. The younger Tarahumara turned away while the elder continued to stare, as if in a meditative trance.

Two AK-47-armed guards appeared at the small window above the door, peered in and grinned.

When Isidrio had finished, Matalo's face was a mangled, bloody mess.

Isidrio swept his gaze to the other inmates as Matalo lay groaning on the ground. "Let that be a lesson to you. You fuck with me—that's what you get." He wiped a hand over his mouth and it painted a horrific, ghoulish red sneer.

Behind him, Matalo crawled slowly toward the wall. In between groans and gasps, he tried to stand up, using the cold concrete wall for support.

Isidrio wiped a shirtsleeve along his clown-like mouth, elongating its menace. He bent down and removed his blood-soaked cowboy boot.

As Matalo started to crawl up the wall, Isidrio approached, raising the boot high in the air. He slammed it down toe-first, embedding it into what little remained of Matalo's eye socket. Isidrio then stepped back, grinning, as Matalo, cowboy boot protruding from his head, staggered forward two steps before dropping face-first like a sack of corn on the hard concrete floor. He twitched spasmodically three times before growing still, quite dead.

Isidrio rolled him over, tugged the boot out of the crushed and bloodied eye socket, pulled it on his foot and turned to the guards, who had stopped grinning and were staring fearfully at the carnage. "Hey," he yelled, wiping the bloody scratches on his face. "Can't you see I'm injured? Get me a fucking doctor."

One of the guards averted his gaze, while the other produced a skeleton key and began fumbling with the lock. It was only a matter of time before Isidrio bribed his way out or escaped from the prison. The guards were unprepared to get on the notorious killer's bad side, knowing that to do so would mark them and their families for death.

The steel door creaked open and a guard meekly motioned for Isidrio to put his hands behind his back. Isidrio obliged and a guard cuffed him. They led him out, locking the door behind them.

Jesus removed his hands from his eyes and stared at the pool of blood snaking toward him from the bloody mess that was once Matalo. Matalo was known as a fearless warrior in the Guadalupe y Calvo region of the Sierra Madre. He had lived by the sword and died by cowboy boots. The question was, would Matalo's brothers avenge the death when they found out?

Jesus thought the battle had the potential to create a nasty, brutal and murderous feud; which is why he wanted no part of it. If he interfered, the first one marked for death would likely be Gloria Alvarez. And right now, her undying love was the only thing keeping him alive.

The elderly Tarahumara looked at Jesus and pulled down an eye socket with an index finger—Watch out.

The door creaked open. Two guards entered and dragged the lifeless corpse of Matalo out, trailed by a wet, red smear.

An old man dressed in tattered blue coveralls appeared, scraped up bits of skull and gray matter into a dustpan and deposited them into a steel bucket. He wheeled a mop into the cell. An armed guard stood in the doorway. The old man mopped up the mess, smiled and bowed at the prisoners, bid them a good day and left. The door closed with a loud metallic clang.

An inmate shrieked from an adjoining cell. It echoed through the corridor eerily. There was another horrible scream and then the unmistakable thwacking sound of fists connecting with faces.

The shafts of light pointing in through the small window painted fiery orange lines across Jesus's somber face. Dusk was snatching away the day.

To anyone else, it might be hell on Earth. To Jesus, the end of one day meant the beginning of another; one less day he would have to wait before he could be with Gloria. But he was growing tired of this impoverished existence. Killing Rodriguez had taught him a valuable lesson. In the Sierra, the weak got their livelihoods snatched away, and were sometimes brutally murdered in the process. Jesus would have to be tougher to survive in this hostile landscape. He would have to prove that he was not one to be trifled with.

He silently vowed that one day things would change—even if it meant turning to a life of crime.

Chapter Twelve

It's not a crime to collect money owed to you over the phone, is it? Depends on how you do it. You threatened him. That's a crime.

Matt's mind was not on Rod Vermooth, the neatly-dressed, clean-shaven middle-aged man with a bad black dye-job and receding hairline—*Is that a combover?*—sitting in his office.

Matt had just finished a dramatic and intense lovemaking session with Angelique, and had started to turn things over in his mind as he returned by taxi to his office. He had yet to call Sal or Sarah, the lawyers. He needed some professional advice—and quick.

He couldn't wait to finish the meeting with Vermooth, even though, like his namesake, the man's mannerisms and word choices suggested an intelligent, professional man—smooth like the aromatized wine.

But Matt was thinking of the threats he had made to property manager Rick Folly over the phone recently—particularly the drunk-dialing threats. He hadn't been as smooth as Vermooth. Matt knew Detective Lyons would be snooping around soon and asking questions. Lyons likely had done some background checks on Matt and learned about the threatening calls—a propensity for violence and an explosive temper. That didn't look good.

As Vermooth delivered his eloquent soliloquy, another question popped into Matt's head. A question he had forgotten to ask Angelique before he left. How was Liberty killed? Matt had noticed a rather expensive cooking-knife collection on her kitchen counter—well-polished and sharpened—and wondered if a knife was the murder weapon. He didn't yet know why the answer was so important. He just knew it was.

Vermooth paused and picked up a letter opener on Matt's desk. He twirled it in his hand, examining the company logo and dull silver blade. It caught a ray of sunshine beaming through a crack in the chocolate-brown venetian blinds and glinted. The reflection caught Matt's eye, momentarily blinding him.

Vermooth noticed and set it down. "You seem very far away. Are you following everything I'm saying?"

"Sorry, I just drifted for a second there. I got it, though." Matt hoped he would get the recap right. To not pay attention to your client's real estate objectives and goals was a cardinal sin in the industry. They were entrusting you with perhaps the biggest investment of their lives. Understanding their needs, showing them options that delivered, was key to a successful relationship. People don't care what you know until they know you care. And Matt needed money—badly. "You were saying you want to start by flipping properties, mainly in the Kitsilano area, do five or six in the first two years, and then use the profit to move onto rental property acquisition."

Vermooth nodded and straightened his posture.

"You also said you don't want to go higher than a million. Is that right?"

Vermooth nodded again.

"And you say you're good with your hands, have tools and good connections with trades?"

Another nod.

"Do you have a pickup truck?"

"I have access to one."

This next question would be tricky, Matt thought. He wanted to be sure Vermooth could arrange financing without being too pushy or intrusive into the man's personal financial situation. It was a fine line, he knew. But so many people bullshitted about the ability to arrange financing. Half the time, they weren't able to get a mortgage. Matt had no interest in wasting time. He had been down that road before and he was far from a rookie.

"Would you mind giving me the contact information for your mortgage broker or banker?" The question also assumed that Vermooth was even willing to hire Matt. It was a calculated close. "When we do a deal, my office will handle the paper trail to the mortgage specialist. It's a courtesy we do for our clients that'll make your life a lot easier."

Vermooth produced a business card and handed it to Matt. "I won't be doing any financing. I'll pay cash for every property. He's my investment consultant at TD Canada Trust. Joseph Shapiro will confirm I'm good for it, if that's what you're worried about."

Matt was impressed. Vermooth had thought things through and seemed to know where Matt was going with his questions. Matt examined the card quickly and placed it inside the file he had started on Vermooth.

"A few things before we finish." Matt was anxious to wrap it up. "You mentioned Kitsilano is your preferred area. I would suggest there are other neighborhoods where we can make money. There are a lot of investors currently flipping in Kitsilano and sometimes finding good inventory is difficult. Oftentimes it turns into a bidding war and properties sell for over list price. I'm not saying we exclude Kitsilano. We'll keep it in the search. But keep an open mind to other areas. In the flipper game, you never know where you'll find the next deal."

"I'm okay with widening the search criteria. You're the expert. Show me the money."

Vermooth, unlike some other wishful-thinking, fly-by-night-flipper-wannabes, knew exactly what he wanted. They discussed time-lines, maximum turnaround time for each project, the utilization of leverage for acquisition as opposed to cash, and a two-tiered strategy that involved the purchase of flippers along with the purchase of revenue properties. Matt provided a detailed analysis of potential net profit on each flip property and also went into detail on Cash-On-Cash Equity Rate of Return.

Finally, Matt could sense Vermooth was hitting information overload—or he had become anxious to leave for his own reasons. But he had begun shifting in the chair, ever so slightly, an obvious clue that he wanted to wrap things up.

Matt stood up, producing a brochure that outlined his services and briefly explained his get-rich real estate investment plan. He would never give away his trade secrets in a brochure for some lesser-skilled bonehead to copy and hang up a competitive shingle. The business was competitive enough without spoon-feeding your trade secrets to competitors. He handed the brochure to Vermooth. "Leave the rest to me, Rod. When I find something, you'll be the first to know. And I won't call you unless I've already previewed the property, crunched the numbers and assured you a profit. And, think about leverage and the acquisition of rental properties also. You don't have to dump a million on each property. Finance them and buy more."

Vermooth extended a hand and Matt shook it. It was clammy and Matt had to fight an initial urge to recoil.

"For now, I don't think I'm interested in rental properties or a mortgage. I'm conservative when it comes to financing," Vermooth said. "But if I change my mind, I'll let you know."

Matt walked Vermooth to the door. "Thanks so much for giving me the opportunity to help you. You won't be disappointed."

Vermooth smiled a smile that said let's see about that, and left.

For five minutes, Matt scribbled notes on Vermooth's objectives and his own gut instincts on the man. *There's something weird about him that I can't put a finger on. Maybe it's just my imagination?* He closed the file and started dialing Sarah.

The office intercom squawked. Michelle's voice chirped, "There's a Detective Lyons waiting outside to see you. Says it's important."

Matt struggled to compose himself. To decline the meeting would immediately arouse suspicion. But to see Lyons would also arouse suspicion. It was a polylemma he didn't immediately have an answer for. "Tell him I'm in a meeting."

He dialed Sarah and got her voicemail. He hung up without leaving a message, dialed Sal, and got him on the phone.

"Matt, I wanted to talk to you about the other day."

"Never mind that now. I need your help. I've got a homicide detective waiting outside my office wanting to talk to me in connection with a murder."

"Did you kill someone?"

"Of course not. Tell me what to do."

"Give me ten minutes. I'll be right over. Keep him in the waiting room. Don't say a word to him."

Matt hung up. The door to his office swung open and Lyons walked in, Michelle right behind, saying, "You can't go in there."

Lyons stood six feet tall, about 210 pounds with a slight beer belly. He wore black polished shoes, blue jeans, a black blazer and a white button-down collared shirt. He had shoulder-length grayish-black hair, a black goatee and brown inquisitive eyes. In his mid-forties, he looked more like a hippie midway through a transformation into a yuppie than a homicide detective.

Lyons ignored Michelle and sat down, eying Matt, searching for a tell of any kind. "I thought you were in a meeting?" Lyons asked.

Matt put the phone in its cradle. "It was a teleconferencing call," he lied.

Lyons held out a hand and offered a disarming smile. Matt shook it.

"I assume you already knew who I am and why I'm here," Lyons said, slowly gazing around the office.

Michelle motioned to Matt—should I stay or should I go now? Matt waved her to a seat beside Lyons.

"My lawyer's on his way over," Matt said.

"Your lawyer? Why do you need a lawyer? You do something wrong? Am I accusing you of anything?"

"Listen, Mr. Lyons ..."

"Call me Ben."

Matt knew he should keep his mouth shut, but couldn't help himself. "Listen Ben, I talked to Angelique earlier. She said you wanted to talk to me about the murder of Alex Liberty. I don't know him and I didn't kill him, for the record." Matt was about to say more but bit his tongue.

Lyons swept his gaze around the desk. His eyes stopped at the letter opener. He stared at it for a few seconds before responding. "Who killed him then ... your girlfriend, or ex, whatever she is?"

Matt paused. Was Angelique capable of murder? What did he know of her background, really, other than what she had said about her previous marriage and her abusive father in Mexico? Was any of it even true? But, if he said nothing, wouldn't that cast suspicion on her immediately? He wished Sal would show up soon and rescue him. He felt like he was digging his own grave. *Why don't you just keep your mouth shut?*

"You think she did it?" Lyons asked.

"I'm sure Angelique wouldn't kill anyone."

"Really? How long have you known her?"

Matt didn't answer the question. "I don't think I should say anything else until my lawyer arrives."

"You need a lawyer?"

"No, but ..."

"But you have one coming," Lyons finished. "Let me ask you something else. Where were you at 9:15 last night?"

"I was at home in bed. I had an accident and suffered a concussion."

"Oh ... an accident. What kind of accident?"

"It was a car accident a few days ago. It's all verifiable."

"Can you verify that you were at home last night ... Anyone who can confirm it?"

Matt thought. He had been at home alone. But wait. He had made some phone calls from his landline at about that time, had he not? He couldn't remember. "I was suffering from a concussion so my memory is a little vague. But, I'm sure I made some calls from my home phone last night. Phone records will confirm it."

"You did," Michelle said. "I talked to you at nine-fifteen."

Lyons ignored Michelle. "Your memory is vague," Lyons said. "We hear a lot of that. Do you remember that Angelique dumped you the afternoon before the murder? Do you remember recently making harassing and threatening calls to a property manager called Rick Folly? He remembers. He's pressing criminal charges and I hear he's also suing you in civil court for damages. Do you know that Angelique had a one-night stand with Alex Liberty just before the murder? Do you know he died of multiple stab wounds, his face slashed beyond recognition? That one, you'd remember, eh? I don't think you could forget that."

Matt felt his face flush. "I didn't kill ..."

"Enough." Sal stood in the door, red-faced, eyes narrowed to slits.

Matt had never seen his friend so angry. Sal was generally a model of diplomacy and composure.

Sal stormed into the office and eyed Lyons. "Who are you?"

"Detective Ben Lyons ..."

Sal could barely contain his rage. "Well, Mr. Lyons, unless you're charging my client with something, I want you to leave this office immediately." He produced a business card and handed it to the detective. "If you have any questions of my client, you go through me. You understand?"

"This was just a casual convers ..."

"Don't give me that bullshit, detective. I know the games. You're trying to get my client to incriminate himself. Get the fuck out of here—please and thank you."

The detective stood. Michelle, with a sweet curtsy, motioned Lyons to the door. "I told you not to barge in here."

The detective looked at her contemptuously.

"You'll be hearing from me," Lyons said, turning to Matt. "I don't know who's crazier—you or that fucked-up girlfriend of yours. Whatever you do, don't leave town."

"That's enough, detective," Sal said. "You'll be hearing from my office. I expect full disclosure before any more questioning. And before you talk to my client, I want forty-eight hours advance notice. And that's not to say I'm going to fucking agree to questioning."

Michelle saw the detective to the door. "You have a nice day now. And please make an appointment with Matt's lawyer next time." She slammed the door behind him and grinned.

Matt held up ten fingers to Michelle. She nodded and left the office, while Matt closed the door and Sal sat down. The throbbing vein in Sal's forehead gradually subsided and some white returned to his face.

"Thanks for that," Matt said, sitting down. "Wow ... I've never seen you so angry. But I'm glad it came when it did and it wasn't directed against me. I wouldn't want to be on the other side of that wrath."

Sal's breathing was finally returning to normal. "You already were. With that stupid email I sent you a few days ago."

Matt didn't think he would forget the bluntness of Sal's warning regarding Angelique any time soon, but there were more important things to worry about right now. "Forget it."

"Let me explain something. I'm going through a period where a lot of old shit is surfacing. I'm not sure how to explain it, but I've been extremely blunt to many people ... giving old high-school bullies what they deserved, that kind of thing. I'm feeling very good about that bravado, but I also wonder if I should stop and become my old timid self—or maybe something in between."

"Sounds like you're overcompensating."

"I think I've been too polite and timid before."

"I like the new Sal when the anger is directed at Lyons, not me."

A smile slowly crept over Sal's face. "I gave it to him good, didn't I?"

Matt nodded. "It might have something to do with your work, too. I know I've been feeling anger boiling just below the surface with all the shit that's been going on in my life. Sometimes I just feel like swearing and cursing out loud, punching a wall or something."

"I am overworked like shit," Sal said. "For sure that's adding to it." He sighed deeply. "I need a vacation—maybe something more meaningful than a fuck-fest. Anyway, enough of that. Sounds like your problems are much worse than mine. Tell me the whole story, starting from when you met Angelique yesterday afternoon."

"Are you going to represent me if I get charged for murder?"

"Let's cross that bridge when we get to it. Maybe this new bravado can be put to good use. Who knows?"

As Matt slowly recounted the events, he couldn't help the sinking feeling of despair crushing his spirit. His ordered, professional, stable life was going to hell in a hand basket.

And he wasn't enjoying the ride.

Chapter Thirteen

Twenty-four-year-old Gloria Alvarez got a ride home in a brand-new black SUV. The driver, whom she only knew as El Toro, wore shiny gold necklaces and bracelets, an expensive black cowboy hat and polished black cowboy boots. She knew El Toro, a Mafioso, supervised the growth and distribution of opium and marijuana fields a few miles outside Guadalupe y Calvo.

She knew he was unconnected with the rival cartel who had executed her parents for refusing to convert her family's cornfield into a marijuana field. In fact, El Toro's narco-traffickers had raided the rival gang's operation two years ago, cutting a wide swath of violent murder in the process. Now El Toro had the police, army and local politicians on the payroll and ran a profitable, if at times ruthless, operation.

El Toro had assured Gloria two of the men responsible for murdering her parents had been slowly tortured before being executed by decapitation. The third, Isidrio Garza, was still alive. There was a complicated truce that currently existed, the details of which Gloria was careful not to ask about. In this region, too much curiosity could mean a death sentence.

She could tell from El Toro's hard eyes that he had a propensity for violence. She also knew he had killed many men. But he had a soft spot for people living in his community. He took care of them, making sure young girls were kept away from drunken perverts who wouldn't hesitate to rape them, given an opportunity. And most of the rapes went unreported. If they were reported, oftentimes the police would become aroused listening to the details of the story and rape the victim a second or third time just for good measure.

The SUV pulled to a stop in front of a run-down house with a corrugated tin roof. El Toro looked at Gloria concernedly, opened the glove box, extracted a nine-millimeter semi-automatic handgun and handed it to her.

She looked at it like it was a poisonous scorpion. "I don't want that. I don't like guns."

"I want you to have it. You never know when you might need it." He had recently rescued her from an attempted rape late at night a block from the rowdy cantina where she waited tables. Manolito, a known rapist in the area, had ties to some drug cartels that El Toro was unwilling to violate. Otherwise, he wouldn't have hesitated to put two or three bullet holes in Manolito's head when he saw him standing over a helpless Gloria sprawled out on the ground, her dress torn open, exposing naked breasts. She was crying and had a few bruises on her cheeks where Manolito had punched her. El Toro had pulled to a stop, fired two warning shots into the sky, and Manolito had disappeared down a dark alley.

"I don't want to kill people," Gloria insisted, even though she knew El Toro would not take no for an answer.

He opened the palm of her hand and placed the weapon in it. "It's for self-defense. In case Manolito bothers you again. He hasn't been bothering you, has he?"

Gloria shook her head. "I haven't seen him in over a week."

He squeezed her hand around the weapon. "We'll you take this, in case you do ... in case he tries anything again."

"Thank you, El Toro." She knew how much he liked being addressed by his nickname. She kissed him quickly on the cheek, put the gun in her purse, and stepped out of the vehicle. "And thanks for the ride."

"No problem. Tomorrow I'll show you how to use it. You take care now."

To the sound of dogs barking, chickens clucking and neighbors snoring, she waved goodbye to El Toro, and entered her adobe-style home. Gloria shared the ramshackle flat with two other young women, both of whom were out turning tricks on the main street. Elvira Sanchez and Abelena Pena, 15 and 16 respectively, plied their trade at odd hours and often hit the streets together to watch each other's backs. They were exceptions to the rule. Most of the young women of the Sierra Madre were married with kids at that age.

Good, Gloria thought. *I've got the house to myself.* Seeing El Toro always reminded Gloria of her parents. Inevitably, her thoughts would drift back to her older sister, Angel, and what had become of her. In the past, she had tried searching for Angel on the small laptop computer the three women shared. Her efforts thus far had produced nothing. But seeing El Toro had planted fresh seeds of curiosity in her troubled mind. And right now, she would do almost anything to take her lovesick mind away from her incarcerated boyfriend, Jesus.

She sat down at the kitchen table, turned the laptop on, and logged into her Facebook account. She searched "Angel Alvarez" and ten results appeared. None of the women resembled what she thought her sister might look like now. *What if she doesn't have the Alvarez surname?* She typed Angel and twenty-six results appeared—again, none resembling Angel.

For the next half-hour, she played around with different name combinations. Scrolling through results for Angelique, she stopped suddenly at an image of a woman who looked eerily similar to herself. Angelique Augusto, now living in Vancouver, BC, had three hundred and sixty-four Facebook friends. The dates and times of photos and posts showed an active, if not habitual, user.

A tingly, excited feeling coursed through Gloria's body and she had to rub the goose bumps flat on her arms. She copied the image of Angelique to her desktop and compared it to her own stored image. The familial resemblance was remarkable. She sighed deeply, tears welling up in her eyes. "That's my sister."

A mangy dog stopped at the half-open doorway, peered in and barked—*roop roop roop*—as if in response. Gloria leaped out of the chair, closed the door and quickly returned to the computer, giddy with anticipation. *Angel. I've finally found you ...*

She clicked on the add friend button and typed a message: *Angel, how are you? I'm Gloria and I think we're sisters. Please contact me soon. I miss you so much.*

Her heart pounding with nervous excitement, she quickly sent the friend request and waited five minutes. No response, but Gloria was not dismayed. Her shift at the local cantina didn't start for another four hours and she silently vowed to wait at her computer until Angel responded.

The only thing she wanted more than to see Jesus freed from prison was to reunite with her sister.

*****

It was early evening and Angelique and Matt lounged leisurely on Angelique's bed, propped up on pillows, sipping wine, listening to hissing traffic and pelting raindrops outside. Intermittent swishing sounds—as vehicles splashed through large puddles—punctuated their serious conversation.

Angelique's blanket had fallen down to her waist and her substantial breasts glowed yellowish-brown from the soft light of the small bedside lamp. Gray shafts of light beaming in from the streetlight, dispersed by the rain, added to the collage of colors dancing across her enormous bosom.

They had just finished a two-hour hotly passionate lovemaking session. Matt listened to Angelique talk, concentrating hard to avert his gaze from the delicious melons twelve inches from his face—each breast was as big as his head, he thought, if not a little larger.

He was beginning to think round two would be forthcoming soon, but Angelique's sudden sullen mood swing had precipitously caused the ship captain to lower the sails—the ship was no longer at full mast. This was serious shit.

They had just recapped the situation involving the murder of Alex Liberty, and how there was a good chance one—if not both of them—would be charged for murder. Angelique had insisted she was innocent and Matt believed her. But suddenly her mood had darkened.

"Sometime I wish I wasn't even born," Angelique said. "Living is so difficult."

"I'm glad you were born," Matt said, putting a comforting arm gently across her flat stomach. "You shouldn't talk like that."

She gazed out the window, sipped her wine and set the glass on the end table. "I've tried to be happy. I've tried so many things to be happy. But it seems all of them just turn out all wrong."

"Things will get better." Matt couldn't help but wonder if her comment was a reference to their relationship, but decided not to mention it.

She dismissed the encouragement. "Sometimes I feel so sad, like I'm going to die of sadness. Sometimes I don't know what to do with my life. I need to find the meaning of my life. I can't see the sun. I feel sad. I want to die."

Matt set his wine down, moved closer, spooning Angelique. "Honey, you have to think positive. We have to figure a way out. When you're down in the dumps, your logic becomes flawed."

"Are you happy? Do you know any happy people? What are they like?"

"I'm not happy all the time. Who is? But I try to keep a positive attitude. If I didn't, things would be a lot worse."

"Sometimes I feel that I'm not very happy generally. And that's my problem."

"I'm sorry you're sad."

"I want to be different. But nothing works. I hate to be as I am. Look at the mess we're in now."

"We'll get out of it."

But Angelique was on a downward mental spiral and needed to get it off her naked chest. "I want to hear things that make me happy, do things that make me happy. But nothing makes me happy."

"I don't make you happy?"

She smiled briefly, an infectious smile that lit up the room, in spite of the somber vibe permeating it. The smile disappeared as quickly as it had appeared. "Sometimes I just want to explode. It hasn't been my week. I don't want to be here or anywhere. Sometimes I just want the land to swallow me up."

"You'll think differently tomorrow. It's been a rough week, that's all."

"Tomorrow I'll have more problems." Angelique had learned about some of Matt's pending civil litigation. "You'll have more problems." A tear welled up in her eye and she brushed it away. "Sometimes I just want to cry. Sometimes I just want to die. Sometimes I want to commit suicide."

Matt kissed her cheek and gently stroked her face. "Please, honey ... don't talk like that. I love you."

"You love me?"

"I love you."

"You know how I am—dangerous and unstable—and you still love me?"

"No one's perfect. You're in my heart, for better or worse, and I love you." Matt was trying not to give away his sudden alarm at the word "dangerous." And he wondered on some level if this was love or lust. *The quickest way to a man's heart is through his dick.*

There was a long pause as Angelique contemplated Matt's words. She half-smiled, erasing the pout. Then darkness overcame her exotic features. "I just want to run away from everything."

She got out of bed, put on a silk black teddy and left the room.

"If you do, take me with you," Matt said, wondering how this roller coaster ride would end. *Crash and burn?*

A minute or so later, he heard a shrill scream from the living room, leaped out of bed, and rushed to Angelique's side. Tears of joy streaming down her cheeks, Angelique stared at the image of a smiling, attractive woman on her Facebook page.

The roller coaster goes down, the roller coaster goes up, Matt thought.

"Look," she said, pointing to the screen. "Who do you think that is?"

Matt stared at the screen for a few seconds. "It's you."

"No, Matt. It's my sister. I think I've found my sister."

He did a double-take. The resemblance was uncanny. They could almost be twins. "I didn't know you had a sister."

Angelique explained her recent visions and dreams of a life much different from the torturous and abusive situation she had grown up in—a Tarahumara Indian existence that was simple and happy, focused on love, family, food, and spirituality—living off the land without the trappings of modern-day civilization.

"In my vision, there was a younger girl. We were playing in a cornfield and I suddenly disappeared. It's always bothered me. I think I might have been kidnapped."

Matt stared at the picture. "Could she be any of your other siblings from San Agustinillo?"

"No. They don't look anything like me. None named Gloria, either."

Angelique returned to the computer, quickly accepted the friend request and typed a message: *Gloria. I've finally found you. Or you've found me. You've made me so incredibly happy. I hope you are well. I have to see you. Get back to me soon. I love you. Angelique*

Noticing two pictures on Angelique's Facebook of her hugging different men, one who looked distinctly Italian, Matt swallowed hard, forcing the green ball of jealously down into the pit of his stomach, where it would hopefully be dissolved and destroyed by stomach acids. *Don't open your mouth. Don't ruin her happiness.*

Angelique rose, spun around, and enveloped Matt in a bear hug. "I love you."

Matt returned the hug and slowly withdrew. He was confused. "What about the doom and gloom earlier?" *Why mention it? You're just giving it life. Shut your mouth.*

Angelique dismissed it like the minor annoyance of an unpaid bill and smiled—that radiant smile that so endeared Matt to this enigmatic and passionate woman. "Oh, forget about that. That was just a bad day, a bad moment, whatever. I'm perfectly fine now."

"You're fine now?"

"Totally. Let's go see her. Come with me to Chihuahua. I need to meet my sister."

A torrent of thoughts swept through Matt's mind. The ups and downs were making him slightly nauseas. Maybe the green ball was growing instead of shrinking? He plopped down in an armchair. "You want to leave the country? We're being investigated for murder. I have tons of financial problems, other pending litigation."

"All the more reason to go," Angelique insisted, perching a shapely butt on the arm of the chair. "Who knows what the future will bring?"

Chapter Fourteen

Rod Vermooth—aka Bob Bolder—knew what the future would bring as he peered through binoculars, watching the kissing couple through the window of the second-floor apartment. The future would bring two murder convictions and incarceration for Matt, and it would bring a violent death to Angelique. Matt would take the fall for both murders.

He grinned with satisfaction. If Matt got too bright for his britches, the plan would change and he too would wind up dead. Fuck the murder charge, even though Vermooth knew that by now Detective Lyons would be analyzing the blood sample Vermooth had planted on the letter opener in Matt's office. Vermooth had guessed right on the detective's instincts. He had seen the detective in action in the past, fooled him on two previous righteous killings—one in which the wrong perpetrator was spending life in prison for the first-degree murder of an attractive twenty-two-year-old woman who had the misfortune to snub Vermooth on the dating site Lavalife.

Vermooth had his strengths. He studied his victims and his pursuers extensively. He was successful because most of the time, he knew what they would do before they did. Vermooth knew Lyons would see the red spot on the letter opener, steal it from Matt's office and discover the sample was a perfect blood match for the now-deceased Alex Liberty, Vermooth's last victim. Liberty hadn't been part of the initial plan. He had just been in the wrong place at the wrong time. Vermooth had been doing surveillance on Angelique's apartment—hatching a plan to kill her—when Liberty had spotted Vermooth hiding behind a car as he exited the apartment after the fatal one-night stand.

Since Vermooth had been made, Liberty had to die. Thinking back on the killing, Vermooth realized it hadn't been necessary to slash him up like he had. But if he had to be completely honest, he knew that a twisted jealously—Vermooth had a sick infatuation with Angelique—had caused him to react with an uncontrollable and violent rage, something not usually part of his modus operandi.

His hands tightened on the binoculars as he saw Matt and Angelique return to the bedroom for sex-session round two. *Fucking bitch. If I can't have you, no one else can. Oh, but I will have you. I'll show you what a real man is like just before I kill you.*

Angelique's chat message flashed into his mind. He had it memorized, indelibly etched into a sick but photographic memory.

> *No, you weren't lying. But, just so you know, I've sent the image to Plenty of Fish administration and plastered it all over the web with a warning to stay the fuck away from Bob Bolder. It's a good thing you hide behind a fake name you fucking pervert. Otherwise you'd have the cops banging on your door—you internet sexual predator freak. Your trolling days are over. Thanks again for your interest and fuck you very much.*

Fuck you very much, he thought. *That's what I'll tell her before I kill her.*

He rolled the window of his black Mercedes up as a passerby glanced over. *Did that fucker see the binoculars? See me?* Vermooth didn't think so. It was too dark, rainy and wet on Denman Street that evening. Pedestrians—and there were few—were more concerned with one thing: getting somewhere dry. He knew they would be less inclined to observe on such a shitty day.

He stared at the tent growing in his jeans and grinned . He unzipped his fly. This urge had to be satisfied.

But as he began to masturbate, he heard swishing footfalls beside the car. He stopped. Then a sudden knock on the tinted glass window startled him. He zipped up the fly, thrust binoculars in glove compartment, rolled down the window, stifled a grimace and forced a smile.

Detective Ben Lyons flashed a badge and stared curiously at the face of a serial killer. "Excuse me, sir, can I ask what you're doing here?"

Vermooth didn't even stammer. "I just pulled up to have a bite to eat." Vermooth waved to a nearby Chinese restaurant with a sign that said *Bill Kee Chinese Cuisine.*

"I'm afraid we need this parking spot. Police business."

"Oh, what's going on? Am I in some kind of danger?"

"Not at all sir. But please move your vehicle. We need this spot."

"Not a problem. I'll see if I can park in the back. It was full last time I checked."

Lyons nodded. "Appreciate the cooperation. And sorry for the inconvenience." He approached a black Crown Vic stopped in the middle of the street with four-way flashers going, opened the door and climbed in.

Vermooth shoulder-checked and casually pulled out, watching in the rearview mirror as the Crown Vic pulled in the empty spot and parked.

Fuck. I'm getting sloppy. I should have known Lyons would start surveillance right away. He doesn't arrest until he's absolutely sure. Or he thinks he's sure. This called for a radical change of plans. Vermooth made a hard right as his normally-calm face began flushing red. He pulled into the alley, drove up behind Bill Kee's and stopped. A vehicle was just exiting the eight-stall parking lot.

Perfect, he thought. He could watch the action from the plate-glass window of the small restaurant while dining on curry beef brisket on rice. He loved that dish anyway. His mood brightened. Sometimes improvised plans were the best. He knew Lyons had probably recorded the license number and model number of his Mercedes, but it didn't matter. The plates and vehicle were untraceable. There were plenty more where they came from, not to mention the multiple clever disguises Vermooth had at his disposal.

Who knows? If the night goes well, maybe I'll get a high-end hooker from Davie Street.

******

An hour later, Matt stepped out onto Denman Street in the pouring rain. He had forgotten his umbrella again. His vehicle was parked a few blocks away, in the underground parking lot of his condo complex. He rarely used the car anymore. Most of his life was downtown. He glanced around, looking for a taxi.

A man eating curry beef brisket in Bill Kee's restaurant watched Matt for a moment, then returned to his newspaper, adjusting a black baseball cap down to conceal his face.

Matt didn't notice.

Another man in a gray trench coat exited from the passenger door of a black Crown Vic parked across the street. He glanced at Matt, opened an umbrella, and sauntered off. The vehicle signaled and slowly pulled away from the curb.

Matt's mind was preoccupied with dangerous travel and murder. He didn't notice. He started a quick gait, spotted the familiar glow of a Yellow taxi a block later, and waved an arm. The taxi stopped and he got in, soaking wet.

As the taxi weaved through traffic, he wondered what the hell he had just agreed to with Angelique. After lovemaking session round two—the discovery of her sister Gloria had evidently refueled Angelique's carnal passion—he had agreed to accompany her to Chihuahua for a family reunion.

Why? Was it because he had just received the best blowjob of his life? *The quickest way to a man's heart is through his dick.* Matt noticed the taxi driver eyeing him curiously from the rearview mirror and he wiped the smile from his face. *What the fuck am I thinking?*

He was about to embark on a trip to Guadalupe y Calvo, one of the most dangerous, crime-infested areas in Mexico. Run from Lyons, run from civil litigation, run away from his business obligations. Run, run, run. But as crazy as it sounded, the plan had been made.

They had booked plane tickets to El Paso, Texas, departing tomorrow at 9:10 am, where they were to meet a man called El Toro, who would drive them into the lawless Sierra Madre—for a $1,000 fee, of course. But Matt thought the fee was reasonable, considering Gloria had indicated via phone conversation with Angelique that "nobody messes with El Toro, he packs an AK-47 and won't hesitate to use it."

When Angelique had asked who El Toro was, the only explanation she had received was, "He's a neighbor and a neighborhood protector."

That would have to do. In the dangerous Sierra Madre, wasn't it better to be accompanied by someone like El Toro, likely a well-connected Mafioso? Wouldn't other bandits have a healthy respect for El Toro, clear a wide path, if not give him the red-carpet treatment? Or maybe he was on someone's hit list? Matt didn't know, but decided the first thing he would do on his return home would be to do some research on the Sierra Madre and Guadalupe y Calvo. Where were they staying, anyway? That part had not been figured out yet, but Gloria had assured them suitable accommodations would be arranged by El Toro.

A fortified complex surrounded by AK-47-armed guards? Matt wondered as he stepped from the cab, handed the driver a twenty, and walked quickly to his apartment entrance.

******

The black Crown Vic stopped across the street. Detective Lyons watched Matt enter the building. Once Matt was inside, he waved to the driver. "Send unit two to watch the building. I want to make sure he doesn't go anywhere tonight. When unit two arrives, go back to Angelique's and we'll collect Trevor."

Matt closed the door to his apartment, removed his coat, went to the computer and started researching.

He found a quote by Christopher McDougall, author of *Born to Run*, referring to Tarahumara Indians:

> *Left alone in the mysterious canyon hideaway, this small tribe of recluses had solved nearly every problem known to man. Name your category—mind, body, soul—and the Tarahumara were zeroing in on perfection.*

Good, he thought. *Angelique is a Tarahumara Indian. She'll take care of me.*

But, after a few minutes of internet surfing, another recent article from a website called Salem News started his hands shaking uncontrollably:

> *Located in the southern tip of the Sierra Tarahumara, the small municipality of Guadalupe y Calvo is high on the list of violence-stricken places. According to residents, executions are frequent in the town of Guadalupe y Calvo proper as well as in the nearby, smaller communities.*

> *"Every day, there are dead outside of town, on the ranches, many of which are not even reported," recently wrote La Joranda reporter Miroslava Breach. "It's not even well known how many die and who they are..."*

On December 7, terror gripped Guadalupe y Calvo when an estimated 50 gunmen said to be working for the Sinaloa Cartel took over the town, burned homes and killed as many as 11 people.

Many residents then reportedly fled the town, joining the ranks of Mexico's displaced populations.

Local police did not resist the assault, or for that matter did the soldiers stationed in El Zorrillo, an army base situated 15 minutes away from the scene of the attack.

It should be noted that Guadalupe y Calvo has been a notorious narco enclave which has suffered numerous bouts of violence for decades, without effective intervention.

Recent flare-ups in violence- possibly linked to the earlier arrests of two Sinaloa Cartel lieutenants-have likewise destabilized other parts of the Sierra Tarahumara. A month ago, the bodies of Moises Velderrain and three of his sons were tossed on the Creel-San Rafael highway. On December 5, Delfina Rodriguez Gonzalez and her 14-year-old son were murdered in Creel.

A former councilwoman for the National Action Party (PAN), Rodriguez was a local representative for PAN Senator Javier Corral at the time of her murder. Some press accounts have linked the double slaying to revenge over the alleged money-laundering activities of Rodriguez's sister, who has since dropped out of sight.

The upsurge in violence is impacting the daily lives and economy of the Sierra's residents. Cristina Munoz Alcocer, president of the Chihuahua Tourism Confederation, attributed the cancellation of 50 percent of the hotel reservations in the Sierra for this year's Christmas holiday season to violence.

Residents, who are fearful to use their names, assert that narco bands effectively control many of the mountain highways and frequently put up checkpoints where citizens are harassed, robbed and even murdered.

Norma Ledezma, president of the Chihuahua-based non-governmental organization Justice for Our Daughters, contended that criminal groups maintain camps where women are taken and sexually abused.

Public outrage flowed in the aftermath of the killings earlier this month of four women who were believed to have been abducted at one of the illegal checkpoints outside Creel. Two of the victims were sisters: 32-year-old Marisa Aide Diaz Peinado, a supervisor at the Technological Institute of Cuauhtemoc, and her 39-year-old sister Mayra Lorena, who worked as a production manager at a maquiladora plant. Their companions were identified as piano teacher Josefina

Diaz de Rempening and Eliza Diaz Martinez, a retired secondary school teacher.

Challenging government contentions that violence was on the downswing, local priest Javier Avila characterized the multiple murders as part of the "daily bread" of the region. Ledezma criticized the official investigation of the murders of the four women as limited in scope.

"It's a stupidity to say that this is about a robbery when the women were tortured and each found with a gunshot to their head," Ledezma said. "It speaks to the position and control that the cartels have in the Sierra, and the collusion of some authorities."

The activist said indications of a broader violence, against women and against innocent individuals, was sweeping the Sierra, and urged the authorities to issue a gender alert.

Finishing the article, Matt clasped his hands together in an attempt to stop them from trembling. It took almost five minutes of deep breathing before he found the nerve to continue.

He spent the next hour doing research on the Tarahumara and the Sierra Madre before checking his email. He saw a message from Angelique and shuddered, despite the recent passion. *What's she on about now? Wanting to dump me again?*

But Matt's frown evaporated as he read the love poem:

Today I met you again. I do not know who you are or where you come from.

Today I looked at you as if for the very first time.

Today I dreamed about you.

Today I thought of you.

Today I wrote a poem about you.

Today I thought about the future and love.

Today I feel so in my heart, I will say that makes two of us.

Also never, I'll never forget, it is difficult to re-love—illusions fail again as well.

Without you my life would not be as it is.

I love you in every way; in the dark, in clarity, in the cold and heat.

If you leave, my soul will suffer every day because you're not here.

Everything has changed. I'm not the same anymore.

This new love is all-consuming and powerful.

I feel the soft sigh of your mouth.

I feel the warmth of your body.

Sometimes it feels like a dream.

But no, we've found:

Hugs!

Kisses!

Sweetness!

Tenderness!

I love you!

I love you!

A day without you is a day lost and wasted.

Sometimes I'm scared and want to return to those days when you were not here—when you were not in my heart.

But it's too late. It already happened and I'm so weak, silly and vulnerable.

My heart is with you now and forever.

Although we are apart now—you in your house, me in mine—I want you to know that I love you to death so.

I love you:

When we're talking.

When you smile at me.

When I sing.

When you write to me.

When you think.

When you look at me.

When I say nice things.

I love your eyes, your hair, your skin, I love your whole way of being.

I love you for who you are.

I thank God that you exist.

I thank God for meeting you.

In such a short time, I love you so much. You are the perfect man.

Understand I am not of metal, cardboard or wood. I am emotional. Just know that I love with heart and soul.

I can't wait to see you, hug you and welcome you into my life. You're the best thing that ever happened to me, Matt Green.

If this love is for both of us, it's not going away.

I often think of you and me.

I want to close my eyes and see you kissing me, giving me your passion.

I imagine us being together in a beautiful and peaceful place.

You are the only man who is now in my heart, my true love and soulmate forever.

Hope you like it, Matt. I mean it! Sorry about the mood swing earlier. Trust me, it was nothing. I can't wait to get on a plane with you. Kisses, much love, Angelique ☺

Chapter Fifteen

At first Angelique saw only blackness. Then, two small white eyes appeared. Then an elongated misty white mouth with black teeth. The face grew larger than life.

She shuddered.

The mouth moved. "Fear not, my child. I'm here not to hurt you but to educate you."

The language was strange, but she somehow understood it perfectly well. "What do I need to learn?"

"Who you are."

"Who am I?"

"Patience, my child. I'll get to that."

"Who are you?"

"I am Romiel. I am a shaman. I am your family. I want to teach you about your heritage. Will you listen?"

The answers I've been searching for. "Yes. Please teach me."

"You are a Tarahumara Indian. We started off as a peaceful and tolerant tribe. But aggression, from the white man, from other indigenous communities, created distrust among our people. We distrusted the ability of our neighbors to forgive. So we took justice into our own hands. We fought to the death to right a wrong. A murder victim, for example, became the real criminal. Through their actions, threats, or bravado, they came looking for death. The victim ceases to have rights, ceases to be a human being, once they transgress certain standards of behavior. We had to defend honor besmirched, and in most cases that involved the death of the perpetrator."

"You can't distrust everybody?"

"We certainly can't, my Angel. But oftentimes the authorities are of no use to us. Oftentimes, they do not protect us. We also form protection pacts with relatives and neighbors. The tight family and neighbor relations have great importance to us; although some indeed involve drug lords, we maintain a strong loyalty to them. Food, shelter and the protection of one another has taken on great importance. Our once undisturbed way of life has become a modified tribal existence borne of the need to survive, thrive and procreate."

"What about those less fortunate in the protection pacts?"

"For Taruhumara, there is an obligation to distribute wealth for the benefit of everyone within the protection pacts. That means food, shelter and water. Of course corn beer."

"What about good and evil?"

"A tricky question Angel, but an intelligent one. Protection pacts aren't necessarily concerned with right and wrong, good and evil, or justice. We think of emotional closeness and the importance of keeping the solidity of these bonds intact."

Emotional closeness. Angelique's thoughts drifted to Matt and, for some unknown reason, her infidelity with Alex Liberty. "What about right from wrong? Infidelity?"

"Any doubts about the family patriarch's worth as a man can often unleash his wrath. Infidelity by a spouse often leads to death."

"Does that mean I'm going to die?"

There was a long pause. Finally, "That's not for me to say. But, for the Tarahumara, death is not considered an end. It's merely a change where the deceased has passed over to the land of the dead. A land of opposites, night is the day of the dead and the moon is the source of light and heat. Night, death and soul are alive in all ways and the spirits of the dead plant in the winter and harvest in spring."

"What about God? What about the Devil?"

"The Tarahumara God, Onoruame, enjoys indulging in corn beer as much as we do. It is a sacred drink. Onoruame is not always a kind deity. He can be bad-tempered, prone to sending droughts, floods, and plagues at the slightest provocation. It is necessary to sacrifice bulls and goats to him when he is hungry. If we don't, the mountains will crumble, blood will rain from the heavens, the sun will die and the people will waste away in sickness."

"So if God isn't necessarily good, then the Devil isn't necessarily bad?"

"Correct, Angel. Very good. The world of the Devil is not necessarily evil, but tainted through affiliation with non-Tarahumara or the chabochi. The Devil and God, brothers, created the human race. God created the Tarahumara while the Devil created the chabochi. The Devil is therefore as much a life-giver and protector of the chabochi as God is to the Tarahumara."

"So God is watching over me?"

"Yes Angel... but beware the Devil."

Angelique suddenly felt ice cold with fear. "Why? Is he after me? Is he after me?"

Silence. The eyes and mouth shrank into black nothingness.

"Tell me what to watch out for. Please, tell me."

Silence. Total blackness.

"Tell me. What do I need to..."

Angelique woke up suddenly and bolted upright in bed. Her heart pounded. Her t-shirt was drenched in sweat. She struggled to still her heart. It took a moment. *A dream, nothing bad. Nothing to be afraid of. A revelation of who I am. Something good. Very good.*

The bedside clock told her it was a quarter to midnight. *Dozed off. Shit. I better get going.*

After a quick shower, she went into the living room and peeked through the blinds of her second-floor apartment. She saw a black Crown Vic pull out of a parking spot across the street and directly below her window. She watched the vehicle slowly cruise out of sight and thought nothing of it. She was leaving everything behind, for how long was anybody's guess.

She had arranged time off work. The trip called for a return to Canada in two weeks. But in the reckless Sierra Madre, that itinerary could change in a heartbeat.

With the dream fresh in her mind, memories flooded back.

At fifteen, she had taken a train up through Copper Canyon and into the village of Creel, where she had spent three nights in a hotel with a boyfriend ten years her senior. They had taken a day-trip into Tarahumara country, visited some indigenous cave-dwellers and purchased some handcrafted jewelry and a few baskets. She was struck by the resemblance she bore to the people: skin color, eye shape and color, and bone structure. It was remarkable, she had thought.

The elderly woman hocking her wares had immediately identified with Angelique. On seeing Angelique, she had smiled warmly and began a dialogue in Raramuri, the tribe's indigenous language. Angelique had understood nothing. The elder had looked befuddled momentarily, but then quickly changed to a chopped and barely understandable Spanish.

Gazing at cornfields while returning to Creel, Angelique had felt an overwhelming affinity for the land and its people, as if the key to her identity was locked away in that strange and mysterious land. It was as if the cornfields somehow held the key.

She had vowed to learn as much as she could about the Sierra Madre and the Tarahumara. And now with the discovery of her sister, Gloria, she knew it was all true. Angelique was a Tarahumara—her roots, history, and heritage defining who she was and why she acted the way she did. Maybe this new knowledge would help her correct the behavior problems she felt might eventually cause turmoil in her relationship with Matt. She knew one thing—she didn't want to lose him, and would do almost everything in her power to keep him. He was hers now and hers alone.

No one else could have him.

She returned to her bedroom and resumed packing. But her thoughts were on the Sierra Madre and the Tarahumara, and how those influences had shaped her personality. She was starting to grasp at a base level what motivated her obsessions and impulsive, angry outbursts. It was in her genes. She zipped up a suitcase, thinking about the Tarahumara version of God. *I'm a Tarahumara. My God is protecting me and my people, the Devil protects the rest. My people. Where are my parents? Gloria didn't mention them.*

Angelique knelt down at the foot of the bed and raised her hands in prayer. *God, protect me, my family and friends, from enemies. Protect my Matt. Guide our journey with a safe hand. I beg you to protect ...*

Thunk thunk thunk ... thunk thunk thunk.

She started at the thumping sound. Someone was knocking on the door. *Who the hell could that be at this hour?*

She walked quickly into the kitchen, extracted a sharp butcher knife from an extensive collection, and tiptoed to the door, raising the weapon high in the air. "Who is it?"

The voice sounded muffled. "It's Detective Lyons. Open the door, please. Your boyfriend's in trouble."

Does that sound like Lyons? In her rising panic, Angelique couldn't be sure. "What happened?"

"He got hit by a car. Now open the door, we don't have much time." She looked through the peep-hole but wasn't surprised by the darkness on the other side. Lately the landlord hadn't been changing hall light bulbs. It had been getting more difficult to navigate the hallways at night.

She silently cursed and pulled the door open a crack. The chain door lock clinked and stopped its progress. She peered into the darkness and heard a crack as the door sprung open—booted in by the intruder—and smashed her hard on the forehead. She fell back, slamming into the wall and melting to the floor.

Her butcher knife clanged to the floor and slid down the hallway.

Vermooth's reactions were lightning-fast. He entered, slammed the door shut, and attacked, thrusting the knife down hard.

Blood trickling from a cut on her forehead, Angelique grunted and rolled as the blade narrowly missed and imbedded itself in the hardwood floor, twanging like an off-tune guitar string. She slithered up the wall, a gray haze of semi-consciousness obscuring her vision.

While Vermooth got up, she kicked him hard in the head, staggered four steps, grabbed her butcher knife and ran for the bedroom.

He slowly recovered from the blow, retrieved his blade and began pursuit. "Fucking bitch," he said, approaching the bedroom door, which Angelique had slammed shut and locked.

Cell phone, cell phone, cell phone, she thought, frantically searching the room as wood on the bedroom door began splintering with the force of Vermooth's kicks. But she had left it in the living room, along with her laptop. She ran to the window, pried it open, and was about to start screaming when something stopped her.

The bedroom door flew open and Vermooth grinned, an I'd-like-fuck-you-first-and-then-kill-you grin. But it wasn't the grin that infuriated Angelique. No. It was what he said: "'You hide behind a fake name, you fucking pervert. Otherwise you'd have the cops banging on your door—you internet sexual predator freak. Your trolling days are over.' Actually, bitch, *your* trolling days are over. And it's you who has the cops banging at your door."

Angelique turned away from the window, her black eyes narrowing. She raised her knife as Vermooth slowly approached, rubbing his swollen head.

"Bob Bolder," she said.

"In the flesh. How do you like me so far? You sure liked the shot of my dick. Now, you're going to suck it for me, aren't you?"

Angelique gritted her teeth and stepped forward. The fear had been replaced by something else—the need for revenge. The need to right a wrong—take justice into her own hands. She glanced at the glinting silver metal of the butcher knife in her right hand, returned a stony gaze to Vermooth. "Bob Bolder, you've just lost your rights as a human being."

With a fury and quickness she didn't know she possessed, she charged forward, dodged a thrusting blade and plunged the butcher knife deep into Vermooth's right shoulder. His eyes widened as she extracted the blade and he swung his combat knife at her throat.

She stepped back—it missed by an inch—and plunged the butcher knife a second time into his chest. Blood spurted from both wounds, dribbling down his black nylon track jacket.

He swung the blade again and it sliced into Angelique's arm—a three-inch gash that dribbled blood down a naked left arm and onto her black teddy. She ignored it and thrust the blade toward Vermooth's throat.

Beep beep beep ... beep ... beep ... beep.

She stopped suddenly, listening to the honking horn. Someone below must have heard the commotion and stopped. A loud, gruff voice confirmed it.

"Is everything all right up there?"

Angelique glanced at Vermooth, who was now wilting down the wall, smearing the white walls with swirling red lines. *Should I kill him? There's a witness outside. He's fatally wounded, anyway.*

She ran to the window, brandishing a blood-soaked knife that dripped tiny red droplets like a dribbling faucet. In the pelting rain, she could barely see the man standing beside a dark pickup, the driver door ajar, engine still idling.

"Are you okay?" he asked.

She quickly concealed the knife behind her back, hoping he hadn't noticed. She turned her injured arm away from view. "I'm fine. I'm moving, that's all. Packing."

"You sure you're okay?" The man's tone was tight with concern. "You don't want me to call the cops?"

"No, no." Even though it was self-defense, with her luck lately, Angelique felt she would be charged and arrested anyway. She didn't want to take that chance. *The authorities, no good. No protection.*

There was a moment's pause.

"Thanks for your concern, but I'm fine," Angelique said. "I get a little flustered when I pack, drop things, you know how it goes. Along with death and divorce, moving is one of the top stress-triggers in the world."

"Tell me about it," the man said. "Good luck with the move."

"Thanks again," Angelique said as he turned, climbed in the pickup, honked once and disappeared.

She closed the window quickly, drew the blinds and spun around; time to put that low-life out of his misery. *He'll learn the hard way you don't mess with Angelique—judge, jury and executioner.*

But her smile of anticipation slowly transformed into a frown.

Rod Vermooth—aka Bob Bolder—had disappeared.

Chapter Sixteen

"It's time to disappear," Angelique said.

Matt glanced groggily at a bedside clock. "It's three in the morning. Now?" But there was urgency in her tone. There was something she wasn't telling him. The phone conversation had started off calm enough, with Angelique asking if he had read her love poem, to which he had answered in the affirmative. Then she had asked how he liked it, to which he had replied, "It's beautiful. You really have a way with words."

But then suddenly her tone had changed. She wanted Matt to pack, promising to meet him in his apartment lobby in an hour.

"I promise I'll tell you everything on the plane. Let's get out of here. Yes, now! Please, honey, please. We really need to go."

There was a moment's pause while Matt thought. This was a trip he knew Sal, Sarah, and Michelle would not approve of, especially given his current circumstance. But, as insane as it sounded, he had already agreed to it. Most of his things were packed already and he had sent emails to the aforementioned, telling them he would be gone for a few weeks. Really, what difference would a few hours make? If he was to board a plane at nine this morning, he had to get up in three more hours regardless. And he was awake now and sufficiently worried that he probably wouldn't fall back to sleep anyway.

"I'll be in the lobby in an hour." He hung up the phone, dressed and began some last-minute packing.

******

An hour and ten minutes later, Matt drove his Supra through rain-drenched streets, navigating his way to the airport. He had planned on taking a taxi, but Angelique had insisted on the Supra, even offering to pay the two-week storage fee at the park-and-fly. Angelique glanced around nervously as they drove.

Particularly after his brief research into the lawlessness of the Sierra Madre, Matt was getting a little scared. It didn't help that Angelique had a bandaged head and wouldn't say what had happened to her.

After a few minutes of driving, he couldn't help glancing around nervously at every passing vehicle, every perfunctory glance from motorists. Finally, his curiosity and fear got the better of him. "Are you going to tell me what happened? If I'm in danger I think I have a right to know."

"It's complicated."

"Well uncomplicate it. Why are we in such a hurry?"

"A man attacked me with a knife after you left. Broke in and tried to kill me."

Matt felt the color drain from his face. "What happened? Do you know him?"

After a moment's pause, Angelique rolled up a black jacket sleeve, revealing a bloodstained, skin-colored bandage.

They locked eyes for a second.

"Are you okay?" Matt asked.

"It's just a flesh wound." She rolled down the sleeve. She recounted the assault, omitting the part about making contact with Bolder on the dating site. *Matt just found out about the one-night stand with Liberty. He must have been devastated, even though technically we had broken up at the time. If he finds out about Bolder, he's going to freak out and leave me. That can't happen. Not now. Not ever.*

"So you don't know who he is, then?"

Angelique shook her head, gazing out the window and avoiding eye contact. Then an idea popped into her head. "Wait a minute."

"What?"

"I think he was an internet dating predator, who I met long before we met."

"Come on Angelique. Either you think he was an internet dating predator or you know he was. I want the truth."

"I don't want to hurt you. I love you."

"If you love me—like you say you do—tell me. I can't have a relationship based on lies." A vein bulged in Matt's forehead and—pulsating—snaked its way to his hairline. "If we don't have trust, what the fuck do we have?"

Angelique didn't get a chance to answer. A pickup truck slammed into the Supra's rear-end, its large steel bumper crunching the low-slung sports car and—metal grating and sparks flying—rode onto the trunk.

Angelique and Matt snapped forward on impact, Angelique's head slamming into the dashboard and Matt bracing hard to prevent a nasty head impact with the steering wheel.

He downshifted and floored it. More scraping and crunching of metal before the Supra finally dislodged from the pickup predator, fishtailed on wet pavement, and began pulling away.

Angelique rubbed a growing lump on her forehead as Matt sought out a side street. He had to get off Granville Street, a main artery. "Are you okay?" he asked.

Her eyes rolled around in her head. "I ... I think so."

He glanced in the rearview mirror, noticing the newer gray vehicle rapidly closing the gap. Matt downshifted, veered over the center line into honking oncoming headlights, narrowly missed a large semi-truck barreling toward them blasting an air-horn, and turned sharply down a side street, downshifting and accelerating as the Supra hydro-planed on water-slicked asphalt for a second before the radials found traction.

"We have a head-start," he said, flicking eyes at the rearview mirror. "He's gotta wait for the semi."

"Go to the airport," Angelique said. Her tone was as nonchalant as if she had just suggested a good eatery.

Matt swerved down another side street, found a poorly lit back lane, pulled into it and searched for a hiding spot. He slowed, drove about a hundred yards, and stopped as another vehicle exited an underground parking lot. He gave the exiting driver the right of way and then sped into the underground, narrowly avoiding getting struck by an automatically closing garage door.

He pulled into an empty parking stall, trying to steady his thumping heart. As he parked, he finally heard it, a rubbery scraping sound coming from the damaged rear-end. To the smell of burning rubber, he turned off the ignition.

Matt watched Angelique as his breathing returned to normal. She was calm, focused, breathing normally, the goose egg evidently not a cause for great concern. They heard an engine roaring outside, the sound getting louder. Matt put an index finger to his lips and they waited quietly.

The noise—a diesel engine clacking intermittently—grew louder still until it sounded like the rumbling was just on the other side of the steel garage door. Then the door suddenly whirred up and the vehicle entered.

Matt froze.

Angelique calmly turned around, reached into the back seat, unzipped a suitcase and pulled out a can of pepper spray and a sheathed combat knife. She unsheathed it, craning her neck to see the vehicle. "Did you see the color of the vehicle that hit us?" she whispered.

Matt willed his dry lips to move. It was an effort. "I think it was gray."

She sighed. "This is a blue truck with no front-end damage."

Was that disappointment in her tone? Matt thought. He had witnessed little of Angelique's anger previously, had only seen one side of it—the cold, standoffish, pouty side. But he suspected a much darker side to this mysterious woman, lurking just below the surface—a dark side capable of spewing violent black venom. He hoped he never got on the wrong side of that wrath.

The blue pickup parked nearby. They ducked down while the driver exited the vehicle, walked to a door marked with a glowing *EXIT* sign, and disappeared.

They waited in silence for a few minutes and heard nothing.

Angelique returned the weapons to the suitcase. Matt faced her. "Do you want to tell me what the fuck is going on now? You almost killed a man—maybe you did kill him—and now someone's trying to kill us. I think that gives me some right to an explanation."

"I wish you wouldn't yell at me. It hurts me when you yell at me." She turned her head away, staring at the rain-soaked window, pouting.

Fuck. The standoffish anger. "I'm sorry, honey. I didn't mean it. It's just that we're in a lot of trouble and I'm a little freaked out right now. Please understand."

Matt waited a minute or so, but the silence continued.

"Give me a kiss," he said, to diffuse the situation.

"I don't want to right now."

Matt had learned the hard way that if you persist in trying to create conversation with a reticent, angry woman, the situation only worsens. The best thing to do, according to his limited and oftentimes confusing experience, was to let them cool down on their own—give them space regardless of how long it took.

He opened the car door. "I'm going to check the damage."

Angelique said nothing.

He left the Supra and examined the damage. The impact had crunched the back-end so badly that the right rear wheel well had been pushed into the rear tire. It had been rubbing up against it and chunks of rubber had been stripped off, leaving little divots. *That would explain the burning rubber smell.* Matt struggled with the trunk, finally managed to open it, and pulled out a crowbar. After a few minutes of wrenching and twisting—grunting but consciously avoiding the use of profanity for fear of upsetting Angelique—he was finally able to find a leverage point that allowed him to free the fender from the tire—only a half inch or so, but probably enough to get them to the airport. It was either put on the spare, which Matt was not inclined to do now, or take his chances with a very unsafe-looking tire.

Fuck it, he thought, jimmying the trunk secure with a piece of rope. *We made it this far. If there is a God, let's hope he's on our side.*

He climbed into the vehicle and glanced at Angelique.

"I'll finish the story later. I promise," she said softly. She kissed him and slowly withdrew. "I have a question."

"Oh? What's that?" Matt asked, starting the engine.

"Have you ever had a blowjob on a plane?"

Chapter Seventeen

Relieved and grinning, Matt de-planed at exactly 1:06 pm, Angelique following close behind, wiping her satisfied face with a tissue. There had been some knowing looks, smiles and scolding glances from other passengers. A pretty female flight attendant had looked amused at the erotic adventure, even offering Angelique bottled water and a tissue when she had finished.

Under the pretense of explaining a movie plot, changing names where appropriate, Angelique had brought Matt up to speed on current events. The realization they probably had a psychotic sexual predator hunting them down and they were likely both wanted by police for questioning—if not murder charges—in connection with the death of Alex Liberty had caused a knot of tension to tighten in Matt's stomach.

Angelique had also gone into descriptive and graphic detail about the abuse she had suffered at the hands of the man who claimed to be her father and detailed other abuse, including rape, at the hands of Mexican machismo ex-boyfriends. The sad revelations had left Angelique teary-eyed and a bad taste in Matt's mouth.

But some time later, Angelique's expert oral care had gone some way to relieving it.

Standing in line at US customs and immigration, Matt felt the return of the tightening knot of tension in the pit of his stomach. "We're visiting your family in Chihuahua City, right?" he whispered.

"Right," Angelique said softly, knowing there were video-cameras and microphones everywhere.

"Are you together?" an El Paso customs official asked as they approached the customs and immigration booth.

They nodded.

He gave them the once-over and scanned their passports. "What's the purpose of your trip?"

"Vacation," Angelique said. "We're visiting my sister in Chihuahua. Renting a car and driving across the border."

Matt tried to hold eye contact with the official, displaying his best relaxed and casual pose. He envisioned them both getting hauled to an interrogation room for questioning before being turned over to Canadian authorities for murder charges. In this day and age of modern technology, how long would it take Lyons to realize their disappearance and have mugs posted worldwide for suspected murderers? *We're fucked.*

"Chihuahua City?" the official asked.

They nodded.

"You won't be staying in El Paso?"

"Maybe one night, on our return," Matt said.

"Where will you be staying in Chihuahua?"

"Holiday Inn," Angelique said.

"What's your sister's name?"

"Gloria Alvarez."

The man punched a computer keyboard and scanned the results. "You're Mexican by birth, I see," he said to Angelique.

"Happy to be a dual-citizen," she said. "I miss my country sometimes."

The official removed his eyes from the computer screen and stared at them for a long moment.

This is it, Matt thought. *This is where he says come with me.*

"Enjoy your stay," the man said, waving them ahead. "And be careful passing through Juarez."

They weren't outside in the hot El Paso sun for long when a newer, red SUV pulled alongside the curb and stopped. A Mexican man with slicked-back black hair, a neatly-trimmed goatee, wearing jeans, cowboy boots and a white t-shirt, hopped out and smiled—a smile that said If I like you, you'll be okay; if not, beware.

Introducing himself as El Toro, the lean, muscular man hugged Angelique warmly and squeezed Matt's hand so hard he almost broke it.

Taking his cue, Matt climbed in the backseat and allowed Angelique to sit up front. She had won instant appeal with El Toro. Matt had some work ahead of him.

Driving through El Paso, Matt sat silently with his thoughts while El Toro and Angelique talked about the journey ahead. The conversation was light and cheerful, like a reunion with an old friend. Angelique had that effect on people.

But at the mention of her real parents, El Toro grew serious. "Your sister will fill you in on all that."

"You mean they're not well?" Angelique only had a vague memory of her real parents. According to Gloria, Angelique had been kidnapped at the age of five, which meant Edgardo, the violent-tempered man who had raised her, and perhaps her foster-mother, Alicia, were criminals of sorts, kidnappers who perhaps needed retribution. Well, she was with the right man for that. She had better keep him on her good side.

"Gloria wants to tell you," El Toro said with a tone of finality.

"I love El Paso," Angelique said, glancing out the window. "It reminds me so much of Mexico."

"That's because it used to be Mexico," El Toro snapped. "Before the mother-fucking gringos took it over."

Matt listened to snippets of the Spanish conversation. About a decade ago, he had travelled extensively through Mexico, visiting multiple destinations, including Mexico City, Acapulco, Puerto Vallarta, Huatulco, Oaxaca, even off-the-beaten-path destinations such as San Agustinillo, Mazunte, and Creel, Chihuahua. His Spanish language skills were good, though maybe a little rusty. But he was only half-listening. He had other things on his mind. Like how Angelique seemed to have so much in common with El Toro, who Matt was sure was a ruthless drug cartel enforcer, who would just as soon put a bullet through your head as thank you very much.

But Angelique and El Toro got along like a house on fire.

Now El Toro was smiling again as they approached the border crossing into Juarez, a notoriously dangerous and violent city that had witnessed all manner of brutal murders, many related to drug cartel turf wars. Matt had read about it online the night before. Referred to by many as the murder capital of the world, 2,086 homicides were reported in 2011 in Juarez and, due to the suspected victory of a drug cartel, that murder rate dropped over sixty per cent in 2012, with only 751 homicides being reported.

Either way, that means two people are murdered every day, Matt thought.

There was also an epidemic of unsolved female homicides in Juarez, most of them involving young woman of impoverished backgrounds and students sharing similar physical characteristics: slender, dark-skinned, and dark-haired. Since 1993, more than 400 young women were murdered in Juarez and Chihuahua Cities, many of them raped, tortured and mutilated before their bodies were dumped in the desert, garbage dumps or sewage areas.

"Good to be home again," El Toro said as an armed Mexican border official waved the vehicle through without so much as a cursory inspection, a look at passports or a single question.

El Toro turned to Matt as they hit traffic gridlock in the city of about 1.5 million inhabitants. "Do you like Mexico?"

"I do. I've travelled to many parts of your country, and I love it."

"Really, what do you love about it?"

"The people are so friendly."

"Mexicans inherently like to enjoy themselves. We live for the moment. Let me give you a piece of advice while you're here. When we get to the Sierra Madre, if someone offers you a drink, don't refuse. They take a refusal very seriously. It could be a death sentence for you." El Toro burst into a raucous laughter while navigating the gridlock. "You've got a lot to learn."

Matt nodded. *Maybe we'll get along after all?*

El Toro cursed at a motorist who cut him off, flipping his middle finger out an open window. "You fucking bastard! Fucking motherfucker!"

"What's with all the traffic?" Angelique asked. "Is it normally like this?"

"No," El Toro said. "Something happened on Cinco de Mayo."

They stopped at a red light and saw the carnage. A blue pickup truck was riddled with machine-gun fire. A man, his head drenched in blood, was flopped over the steering wheel. The other victim, who had apparently tried to run from the assassin, lay on his back in the middle of the street, beside a passenger door that was ajar. His body and head were riddled with bullets and a puddle of blood snaked out around him. One leg was twisted at an odd angle. Yellow crime scene tape barricaded the scene while police and military examined it for clues. Other AK-47-armed officials directed traffic down a side street.

Matt instinctively ducked down while Angelique surveyed the carnage curiously.

El Toro turned to Matt and grinned. "Don't be scared. It's all over now. And the fucking rival cartel bastards got what they deserved."

Matt popped his head up. "Okay."

"Welcome to Mexico," El Toro said, swerving down an alleyway. "I have a quick stop to make."

They pulled up to a delapitated apartment building where an old woman on a second-floor balcony was beating a carpet with a broom. Plumes of dust dusted the vehicle as they arrived.

The woman waved and smiled, exposing missing, rotten and crooked teeth as El Toro got out. He returned the greeting and turned to his passengers. "I'll just be a minute. Wait here."

Not that they had a choice. He had removed the keys and locked them inside the vehicle.

El Toro disappeared inside the building and returned a short time later armed with an AK-47, a semi-automatic nine-millimeter handgun, a sheathed sword and a combat knife. He also carried a 12-pack of Tecate beer and a package the size of a brick, wrapped in black plastic and taped with gray duct tape. He tucked the package inside a concealed compartment in the back of the SUV and returned to the driver door.

He opened it. "Would you like a beer?"

Matt hesitated momentarily before he felt the gray matter in his brain begin to process information. "Sure."

Angelique nodded quickly and smiled. She was finally in her element.

They drank beer and drove out of Juarez.

Matt was on his third beer and comfortably numb by the time they cleared the city limits and were travelling south down Highway 45 across the sandy desert, marked by the odd cactus, a picturesque glowing sun and artfully windswept sand dunes. They had just blown through a military checkpoint with only a nod and a smirk from the officer who had waved the SUV over. El Toro had even handed a beer out the window, which the sun-stricken soldier had gratefully accepted.

The trip called for a four-hour drive to Chihuahua City, where Matt and Angelique would indeed spend the night at the Holiday Inn. The following morning at 9:00 am, El Toro would pick them up and continue southeast for most of the day, eventually arriving at the town of Guadalupe y Calvo, where Gloria was anxiously waiting for her sister to arrive. Accommodations had been arranged in the small town.

Angelique sipped beer, glanced at the scenery occasionally, and played with her smart phone, while Matt and El Toro talked. Their rapport had improved, due in part to the alcohol. They stopped at a small town at the halfway point, ate some deliciously spicy tacos, bought another 24-pack of beer, and carried on. El Toro had insisted on paying for the beer, so Matt offered only a token gesture of protest.

Fifteen minutes into the last leg of the trip, El Toro started telling Matt his version of the war on drugs. "You know, every time the government decides to make some token attack on the drug trade, the local economy in whatever village they attack drops substantially. The standard of living I'm talking about."

Not the people getting killed, Matt thought. But he wasn't prepared to argue with the drunk driver.

"The government just makes a token effort to satisfy public pressure," El Toro said. "But in the end, they don't want the drugs to disappear. Do you know if drugs were completely eliminated from Mexico, our economy would drop by sixty-three per cent?"

Matt silently drank his beer.

"Go ahead," El Toro said. "Play devil's advocate if you want. I'm not going to shoot you. You're drinking my beer." He burst out laughing, extending a hand. "Give me five. Then pass me another beer, please."

Matt obliged. "So you're saying everyone benefits from the drug trade—police, military, politicians, locals?"

"Look at the Tarahumara," El Toro said, smiling at Angelique. She turned off the smart phone and returned the smile. "No offense—I hear you're a purebred Tarahumara—but they're doing a hell of a lot better growing opium and marijuana than they ever were growing corn, beans, or squash, whatever. Now they can actually send their kids to school, get them proper medical care, increase their quality of life and lifespan. Do you know the Tarahumara average lifespan used to be forty-five, before the cartels came along?"

"What is it now?" Matt asked.

"At least another ten years," El Toro said. "The cartels protect them—I protect some of them."

"What if they refuse to grow marijuana or opium?" Angelique asked.

"That's a different story," El Toro said. "But we don't kill them—not like some cartels have done. We just make the offer so sweet they can't refuse."

"But what if they do refuse?" Angelique goaded the drunk driver with a loaded gun.

El Toro's features hardened. "Listen, do you know how many times I saved your sister from being raped?"

A tense silence followed as the crimson sun began its descent over the vast desert horizon. Matt kicked the back of Angelique's seat and El Toro shot him a scowl before continuing. "At least a half a dozen times. If I hadn't stepped in, Gloria would probably be dead right now and your little family reunion wouldn't be happening. What do you know of life in the Sierra Madre? You've lived in Canada for too long. You know nothing. And you dare to question the methods of El Toro, your sister's protector? Do you think I drove all the way to El Paso to pick you up for your shitty thousand dollars? No. I did it for Gloria. And you don't come near to measuring up to her caliber." El Toro rolled down the window, uttered a guttural growl and spit into the wind.

"I don't think she meant what she said," Matt tried.

"Stay out of this, gringo," El Toro said. "This is not the time to be brave. Let your girlfriend speak for herself."

"I'm sorry," Angelique said. "Your right, I'm being stupid. I've been away from this life for so long I have no idea what it's like. And thanks for looking after Gloria. I promise you have my loyalty now and I'll never show you any disrespect again."

There was a long silence before El Toro finally grinned. "Salud," he said, holding up a half-full beer bottle. "I can't kill you. You're drinking my beer."

They toasted and drank. "I wasn't going to tell you this," El Toro said after a moment, slurring his words. "Ask Gloria to forgive me."

"What's that?" Angelique said.

"Your parents were murdered by a rival drug cartel for refusing to grow marijuana in their fields."

Angelique bent her head into her hands and stayed that way for a long time. El Toro and Matt stayed silent.

Finally, El Toro said, "I killed the men responsible, except for one man."

"My parents are dead?"

El Toro nodded.

"And you killed the men responsible?"

"I did."

"I owe you my life."

"I appreciate that."

"What about the one man?"

"You want him dead?"

Angelique slowly nodded.

"Honey, you can't go ordering hits around here. You don't even know the repercussions," Matt said.

"But I know the repercussions," El Toro said. "And we might be able to arrange something. The man's name is Isidrio Garza, and he recently overstepped his authority in prison. He killed a friend of mine."

Wow, Matt thought. Angelique's relationship with El Toro had switched from flirtatious to adversarial to allies, all in the course of three and a half hours. What would happen to it in three and a half days?

"You mean we can do something?" Angelique said, after a moment's silence.

"Let's not talk about it now," El Toro said. "We're all too drunk and foggy-headed. It might just be the alcohol talking. We'll talk about it tomorrow morning."

The conversation was sparse as they continued the journey. El Toro drove with a focus that said he wasn't interested in talking anymore. Angelique and Matt respectfully took the cue and kept their conversation to a minimum.

Finally, he pulled up to the Holiday Inn in Chihuahua City and dropped them off.

"Tomorrow, nine o'clock sharp," El Toro said. "Don't be late."

Inside the hotel, Matt sat in a lobby hotel chair while Angelique dealt with the room details at the front desk.

Matt turned on his phone, saw five voicemails and a dozen new emails. He scrolled through the emails.

He only had time to scan the titles. The two that immediately caught his eye were from Sal. One said: *I warned you about her*; the other: *Where the fuck are you?*

Chapter Eighteen

"You're ordering fucking hits? We just got here and you want someone dead? Are you crazy?" Matt asked.

They were in the hotel suite. Matt sat on the bed while Angelique brushed out her long hair at a mirrored vanity. She had just finished showering and had a white towel wrapped around her body. Matt talked to her reflection in the mirror.

Angelique frowned, and continued brushing her hair. "I wish you wouldn't call me crazy. That's insulting."

"Sorry." *Acknowledge you're wrong even if you don't believe it. That's the secret to bridging the gap between the sexes.* "It's just that this is ..." *Don't use the word crazy ... and no, not insane either ...* "ridiculous."

"That Isidrio, whoever he is, killed my parents. How do you think that makes me feel?"

"I'm sorry about ..."

"It makes me feel like hell. And it makes me want revenge. Do you know who I am, Matt? I'm a Tarahumara Indian. Do you know anything about the Tarahumara?"

"Not much."

"We're pacifists who turn into fierce warriors in defense of our way of life. The Spanish conquistadors found that out five centuries ago when they invaded Mexico. We attacked guerilla-warfare style from treacherous reaches of the Sierra Madre, which the Spanish were too afraid or physically unable to traverse. Other colonists used us for slave labor while trying to integrate us into European villages. We revolted, in some cases violently."

"Does that justify murder?"

"Try to understand. The key to our survival as a race is to show the chabochi we're not to be messed with. It's also the law of survival in the Sierra Madre. We've survived because of our physical strength and endurance, our ability to venture deep into the canyons and caves, and then attack when the strategic advantage is ours. We want to be left alone, not exploited by outsiders."

"I don't fancy being locked up in a Mexican jail, or getting killed while I'm here."

Angelique spun around in the chair and looked at Matt pleadingly. "We're not going to get killed. El Toro will protect us. Did you see how fond he is of Gloria?"

"Seems to me he could just as easily put a bullet through our heads as protect us. He was on the verge of exploding earlier. Did you see his face? He's a dangerous killer."

"Don't worry. I'll take care of you. I love you. I'm sure Gloria is well-connected. She's survived this long in the jungle."

"Could you at least think about it overnight?"

"Okay, I'll do that. But don't be surprised if I don't change my mind. It's not like I have a choice in the matter. If my mother were alive today, what do you think she'd want me to do? She'd want me to avenge her death, and she'd never forgive me if I didn't. I know how Tarahumara communities think. We didn't create this world of lawlessness. The exploiters and the criminals did. Community chiefs and shamans kept order in the old days. We're just adapting to the new order. I mean, look at the Canadian justice system. People can sue you for anything and they do. And the criminal justice system—innocent people go to jail all the time, murderers walk away scot-free. That's no good. An eye for an eye, that's how it should be. And that's how it is here. The Mexican police will never arrest Isidrio. If he's in jail now, he'll get released soon, if he isn't walking the streets right this minute." In the mirror, Angelique's black eyes were fixed hard on Matt.

But he didn't know what to say. The discussion was making him tired. Events were starting to take a toll. The beer buzz was fading rapidly. Fatigue had crept up and slammed him like a derailed train. And he was hungry.

He looked out the window at the orange sky and checked the time: 7:36 pm. Time enough to see some sights and have dinner, anything to take his mind off the mess he was in. "Are we still going out for dinner?"

Angelique stood up and spun around. She adjusted the towel, affording Matt a glimpse of her ample bosom.

A smile crept across his lips. *Damn, I wish the pirate captain would stop navigating the ship. He's going to sink it.*

"I'd like that," Angelique said, doing a little pirouette, and slipping into the bathroom. "I need some quality romantic time with you."

******

Twenty minutes later, leaving the San Felipe residential area, they walked hand-in-hand toward central downtown and La Casa de Los Milagros, a restaurant recommended by an efficient and cheerful desk clerk. Happy hour was happening at the hotel restaurant and bar, and by all reports the food was good, but Matt wanted some fresh air. He knew they would be returning later by taxi, as the area could get a little dodgy late at night.

Strolling in front of the Metropolitan Cathedral Church of the Holy Cross, Matt admired the colonial architecture dating back to 1725. The desk clerk had proudly informed them it was "the finest example of colonial architecture in northern Mexico and the main ecclesiastical building of the Catholic Church here."

"I thank God every day that I'm with you," Angelique said, kissing Matt on the cheek. "You're my gift from God."

Matt wasn't sure about that. But he had to admit, Angelique looked ravishing in a mid-length, low-cut, body-sculpting black dress, black pumps, and her long, flowing black hair. A white camisole complimented the ensemble. She had assured Matt prior to leaving, "You'll be having dessert at the hotel."

By comparison, he was underdressed with Levi blue jeans, brown leather deck shoes, a white golf shirt and black fleece zip-up jacket.

They arrived at La Casa de Los Milagros a short time later and sat down. Matt ordered chile relleno while Angelique ordered a rare steak with baked potato, creamed chillis, mushrooms and a smoked jalapeño. They ordered two strawberry margaritas to start.

By the time the food arrived, they were on their second round and a sedate alcohol buzz was dulling Matt's senses. *Comfortably numb. Comfortably dumb.*

As they ate, Angelique talked cheerfully, as if they had not a care in the world. "There's something I've been meaning to ask you."

Matt sipped his margarita between mouthfuls of chile relleno. He chewed and swallowed. "What's that?"

She took his hand. "Don't look like that. It's not bad."

"Tell me."

Her dark eyes grew misty. "I love you, Matt. You stole my imagination and I want everything with you. I want the world with you. I hope you love me the same way."

Matt didn't know what to say. He was confused. But he said it anyway. He thought he felt it and it was real. "I love you, too."

Angelique continued: "By God I've discovered I'm so in love with you. I want to keep and cherish this feeling forever. Your love makes my heart beat with warm rhythm and gives me strength. I like that feeling and I want to feel it in my chest for the rest of my life. I think this time I've found my soulmate. I want to continue to believe it's you and only you. I'm so crazy in love I want to paint colorful stars and hearts in the sky. I hope that we're always together and will always be Angelique and Matt, two—and one day, maybe three."

Matt had considered children in the past. He was sure he didn't want to have kids. But he didn't have the heart to bring it up at that moment. Angelique gushed forth passion and emotion like a volcanic eruption of hot, molten lava. He nodded and smiled, feeling the familiar stirrings of desire.

"I've never felt love this powerful," Angelique continued. "I want to kiss that mouth, my mouth, my angel. Our fights only strengthen my feelings for you. I thank God for meeting you, and thank you for making me happy. I want you all for myself and nobody else."

"You make me happy, too."

"I'm so distracted by this love, and sometimes I crave too much attention, get a little crazy, but I feel happy that I'm in heaven. I feel positive about our romance. Let me prove that I am the one for you, that you're not wrong about me. I just want to love, love only you can give me. I know we're going to be together and we will not separate. I pray to God every day that I can keep seeing your beautiful eyes"

"Is this leading to a question?"

Angelique still held his hand. "Let me get this off my chest. I fall asleep and I wake up naked with the feeling that we've made love. I hope you forget the bad things about me and only stay with the good things."

"I try not to dwell on the past. It doesn't do any good."

"It's true, and love is also about forgiveness."

Matt couldn't help but wonder if there was some ulterior motive for this gushing geyser of affection. Maybe she was setting the stage for his forgiveness once she ordered the hit on Isidrio? "Is there something you're not telling me?"

"Of course not. I told you all that to tell you this." Angelique opened a small black purse and extracted two black metal rings.

Matt's eyes popped.

"These aren't engagement rings," Angelique said. "They're promissory rings." She smiled and handed one to Matt. "I've opened my heart to you. I want you as my boyfriend. I hope you love me with the same intensity that I love you. Will you be my boyfriend?"

The emotional outburst, along with the margaritas, had gone to Matt's head. And Angelique absolutely glowed with joy. He couldn't let her down now, especially given the mind—or the bind—he was in. Imagine how it would look to Detective Lyons if he learned they were off again? On again, off again—a rocky road of instability and potholes, a recipe for disaster and maybe murder.

"I will," Matt said. "We were a couple long before I said it: probably when I first laid eyes on you."

She sprang out of her chair and approached Matt. He stood, hugged and kissed her, to the applause and cheers of patrons. Matt put the promissory ring on Angelique's wedding finger and she did the same. They fit perfectly. They held up their hands and patrons applauded, one drunk man even shouting, "Speech, speech, speech."

Even the waiter brought over another round of margaritas. "These are on the house. Are you engaged to be married?"

"Yes," Angelique said quickly.

They sat down.

"I love you, boyfriend," Angelique said. "I like the sound of that."

"I love you, girlfriend." Matt shuddered as goose bumps crawled up his forearms. It was not cold in La Casa de los Milagros.

******

One hour and fifty-five minutes later, Matt sat in semi-darkness on the hotel suite toilet. Shafts of gray-white light seeped through the bathroom window from a streetlight outside. And the screen of his smart phone glowed blue-gray. He and Angelique had just made love a half hour ago and she had drifted off to sleep. Her performance was that of a Greek goddess of love. She had been on fire with passion and lust. Matt couldn't ever remember a time when he had sex as wholly satisfying as that surreal and incredible session a short time ago.

But he was anything but aroused as he read the first email from Sal: *Where the fuck are you?*

> *Matt, I don't know what the fuck you think you're doing, but it's been very difficult for me to keep that Detective Lyons at bay. He said he found a letter opener at the murder scene of Alex Liberty with your company logo on it. He wants to question you and Angelique. I told him you're on holiday, but he says if we don't show up at his office within a week for questioning, he's charging you with first-degree murder. You're in a lot of trouble. Don't do this to me, Matt. Call me when you get a chance. Sal*

Matt stood up, splashed some water on his face, toweled it off and sat down on the toilet again. It was the email entitled *I warned you about her* that worried him the most. Finally he worked up the courage, opened it and read:

> *I should have probably got your permission to do this first, but I went ahead and did it on my own. I know I'm just negative when it comes to women, but I'm only trying to protect you. I'm sorry I was so harsh with you the other day regarding Angelique, but now I realize I was right. I certainly could have put it more diplomatically, but it doesn't take away from my gut feeling on this.*

I set up a fake profile on some dating sites the other day and started surfing around, looking for Angelique. Well I found her on Latin American Cupid. Her profile says she is looking for pen pals and friends, but she also posts her status as single. I thought you two were an item now. You can track user activity on the site and I can tell you that she uses it almost daily. In fact, she was using it just a few hours ago, probably on her smart phone, even though she's with you somewhere in Mexico.

Matt stopped reading and wiped sweat from his brow. His heart was racing. He took a few deep breaths before continuing.

I set up a profile as John Altec, used a bought picture of a forty-four-year-old handsome man with deep blue eyes. I sent Angelique (she calls herself Angel) an interest message and here's the chat conversation that followed. Don't be mad at me, Matt. I was only trying to protect you, not date her or anything. I swear. This conversation went down within the last twenty-four hours. It's a cut and paste job of the original. I've since blocked her from further communication. I don't want to torture you with details of where this might have gone if I let it continue. You've got enough on your plate right now. You've got to dump Angel, get home and deal with your shit.

See for yourself what a loyal and honest woman she is:

John: You are cute. Your picture is very beautiful.

Angel: ??? ☺

John: Thanks for the smiley face Angel. Your picture is very beautiful. I am working in the United States right now but will be visiting Vancouver in a month. I would like to meet you if possible. I hope to hear from you soon.

Angel: Hello, hello, John. It would be great to meet you. If I don't get to meet you, I hope you enjoy your stay in Vancouver. I send you kisses.

John: Thanks for getting back to me. I like your photo. As I said, I will be visiting in a month and I'd love to meet you. I hope you get back to me soon. I send kisses.

Angel: That would be great, John. I also like your photo and thanks for the kisses you sent. ☺

John: Thanks for that Angel. Your photos are beautiful. I'm looking for a girlfriend, as I'm relocating to Vancouver. I hope I can see you when I arrive. I hope you don't have a boyfriend. Kisses ☺

Angel: That's perfect. You're looking for a girlfriend. ☺ Ohhhhhhhh ... you're welcome in Vancouver and I hope you like it. I hope I can see you when you arrive. ☺ I don't have a boyfriend. ☺

John: That's great if you don't have a boyfriend. It's much better if you have no one serious in your life right now and you're not currently in love with anyone. I'm single also. I'm looking for a girlfriend to have a close and special relationship with. I would like to get to know you better, Angel. I would love to buy you dinner and drinks. I send you goodnight kisses. I'll send more messages tomorrow. I hope to hear from you soon. Enjoy your evening. I really like your beautiful smile.

Angel: You make me smile and I send you many kisses. Muuaahh.

John: I'm glad I make you smile, beautiful. I send you many kisses.

The first emotion Matt felt when he finished the email was a deep and painful stinging sensation that started in his heart and spread painful tendrils throughout his body. He put his hands to his face and the smart phone slipped from his grasp, clacked on the floor and slid about three feet before coming to a stop, the screen still glowing ominously.

He sat for five minutes, feeling the pain.

The second emotion he felt was a sense of relief that he knew now instead of finding out later. Now he wouldn't have to deal with this undulating drama anymore. In some ways, it felt like the weight of an elephant had been lifted from his shoulders.

He let mixed emotions of pain and relief settle over his body for another five minutes.

Then his mind went into think mode. Thoughts tumbled like an avalanche. *What do I do about it? Do I confront her with this, down here in Mexico? Do I leave, run for the border and get the fuck out of Dodge? With a fucking hit man watching over us? Are you kidding? Who's to say she doesn't cut him loose on my ass? The law of the Sierra Madre, as she says. Righting a perceived wrong. Mess with me and face my wrath. Hell hath no fury like an angel scorned. Fuck, what to do? Don't make a rash decision. Sleep on it. An answer will come to you. Do you love her? I don't know. Maybe. No. Yes. I don't know. Does she love you? Maybe. No. Yes. What's she doing with you? What's her master plan? Is she just the kind of woman who feels the need for more love and romance and is constantly looking for ways to satisfy those desires? Has her abused past left her always craving love but yet unwilling to trust herself to love me fully? How the fuck should I know? I'm not a psychologist ... For now, do nothing. Go back to bed. What a fucking lying, deceitful, bitch. I could kill her.*

"Honey ... honey are you all right?"

"I'll be right out." Matt flushed the toilet, ran the tap for a minute, splashed cold water on a face flushed red with emotion and toweled dry.

He left the bathroom and approached the bed. Angelique squinted at him through sleepy eyes. "What were you doing in there?"

"Nothing. I had a nightmare and just needed to bring myself down to reality."

"Are you okay?"

He slid into bed and wrapped an arm over her slim waistline. The blanket had slid down and her large breasts glowed gold in moonlight seeping through Venetian blinds.

"I'm perfectly fine, Angel. Never better. Go to sleep. We've got a long day ahead of us tomorrow."

Angel? He's never called me that before, Angelique thought as sleep slowly enveloped her senses. *That's strange.*

Chapter Nineteen

Jesus thought it was a strange signal, but considered approaching the man anyway. He was out in the walled exterior exercise yard of the prison and had been sitting stoic for about an hour with two other Tarahumara: the elder, Javier Romero, who had cautioned him yesterday while witnessing the brutal murder of the Tepehuan, and the younger boy who had also witnessed the murder.

The younger boy had sat with them quietly for about twenty minutes before his youthful vigor won out. He befriended another prisoner and they began a friendly sparring match a few feet away.

Jesus sat quietly beside Javier in a meditative trance. They hadn't uttered a word for almost an hour, displaying that ability the Tarahumara possess for sitting for long periods of time, motionless, speechless and ostensibly inactive. Observers had commented on it and didn't know how they did it, or what they were doing, often mistaking it for laziness. But it was more of a state of connectedness with present, body and mind, a state of just being without doing or thinking, a form of Tarahumara meditation.

The Tarahumara viewed work as necessary for survival, but didn't attach any intrinsic moral value to it outside of that. They placed far more importance on the soul, spirituality, and the depth of the bonds they shared with family and close friends. These values far exceeded any value that work could possibly provide.

To Jesus's mind, he *was* working, hoping to benefit from Javier's inner peace. The violent murder of the Tepehuan Indian earlier had left a visceral and haunting image etched in his mind, as much as he had consciously tried to quash it. But Jesus wasn't much like his Tarahumara predecessors in many ways, in part due to his assimilation into a society based on money instead of barter as a form of existence. Jesus was generations removed from Javier's more traditional beliefs and values. The shaman still wore a loincloth and sandals made from strips of recycled tire rubber. Javier gutted out the often cold temperatures at night with little protective clothing and bare legs.

While Jesus still held to some Tarahumara beliefs, he was not cut from the same cloth as the peaceful man sitting beside him with an impassive expression.

His family, driven from their homeland by the exploiters, was now fragmented, working and living apart for large stretches of the year, trying to earn subsistence living. Jesus's new life was an example of how the traditional way of life of the Tarahumara was slowly being eroded, replaced by an existence with an emphasis on money and earning potential. He lived in squalor and to make ends meet, had to shine shoes in a fierce and competitive market. But now he was in jail, with little or no hope of seeing Gloria for a very long time, if he could even survive the violence pent up inside these walls.

But that was about to change.

From the other side of the prison yard, the mestizo raised his eyebrows at Jesus a second time and pointed to his shoe again.

Javier Romero stirred from his trance-like cross-legged sitting posture and raised an eyebrow. Don't go. Whatever you do, don't go.

But Jesus ignored it. He wasn't feeling any of the shaman's inner peace, anyway. If anything, his psyche felt more disturbed than before he had joined Javier. He stood up in the heat of the mid-day sun and walked over to the mestizo. As he got closer, he recognized the man as Juan Medina, a drug cartel underling, a low-level protector of opium and marijuana fields in a pocket of the Sierra Madre. Juan wore a gold necklace, matching bracelet, new Wrangler blue jeans, spit-polished brown cowboy boots and a matching brown suede cowboy hat. He had a thick black beard, slicked-back black hair, and spoke in a deep baritone voice. "Boy, your shoelace is untied."

Jesus knew he would have to choose his words carefully. Engaging in conversation alone might cause rivals to wonder at the intrusion to the territorial hierarchy of the prison system. Jesus looked at his black Nike running shoes, an afterlife-gift from the late Rodriguez Sanchez. He noticed the laces were not untied. But he strolled to within five feet from where Juan stood with five others in his clan and bent down, feigning shoelace tying.

Juan distracted the group with a loud chuckle while pointing to the sky, and tossed a folded white piece of paper the size of a postage stamp tied with an elastic band. Jesus picked up the paper and returned quickly to his spot beside Javier. As Jesus opened it, he glanced at Juan, who discreetly flashed him the thumbs up.

Out of the corner of his eye, Javier watched as Jesus held the paper discreetly between his legs and slowly opened it.

Javier raised an index finger and a scowl crept across an otherwise expressionless face.

Jesus ignored Javier and read the message:

El Toro is bringing Gloria's sister, Angel, to town this afternoon. El Toro and Angel want Isidrio dead. He killed Gloria and Angel's parents and disgraced the honor of our group. Kill Isidrio and we guarantee instant release from prison and protection from Isidrio's group. There's a shank in the wall beside east entrance. Black handle protruding. Do it now.

Gloria does have a sister, Jesus thought. *And she wants Isidrio dead. And so does El Toro. Isidrio killed Gloria's parents. Gloria is my family. Angel is my family. I want to be with Gloria. I want to meet Angel. I want to better my life.*

It wasn't a difficult decision.

Javier scowled as Jesus stuffed the message in his mouth, chewed and swallowed it. Then he stood up and slowly made his way over to the east entrance, where Isidrio leaned against a wall, having an animated conversation with three allies.

Isidrio's black eyes darted away from the group and followed Jesus. The conversation stopped.

Juan's group grew silent and slowly approached Isidrio.

The two young prisoners continued their phantom boxing match.

I can't do this now. He's watching me. Do it now. Gloria. Gloria. Do it for her. Jesus reached the east entrance, scanned the wall for the black protrusion and spotted it. He quickly leaned against the wall, feeling the black taped handle poking his shoulder blade.

Isidrio approached to within about thirty feet. "Hey boy, what are you doing over here? Get back to your corner of the yard."

"I need to be alone with my thoughts."

"No, you don't."

"Yes, I do."

Nearing, Isidrio unsheathed a knife and brandished it. "Do you want this? Didn't you see what I did to the Tepehuan son of a whore who disrespected me?"

When Isidrio got to within three feet of Jesus, Juan shouted to him from the middle of the yard. "Hey you, tough guy, what do you think you're doing?"

Isidrio's head turned toward the threat, scowling.

It was the distraction Jesus needed. He spun around, grasped the handmade shank, and lunged toward Isidrio, plunging the blade down.

Isidrio side-stepped a little too late. The blade's knitting-needle shank penetrated his chest. Isidrio winced and swiped his knife at Jesus.

It sliced a gash in the side of Jesus's neck. Jesus ignored the blood spurting out, extracted the blade and stabbed Isidrio again in the chest.

Prisoners formed a circle of death, some cheering the combatants on, while others silently watched. Three AK-47-armed guards stood at the south entrance and watched, unwilling to intervene. Let the prison hierarchy take care of itself. It always did.

Jesus extracted the blade and lunged for a third strike, but a powerful left hook connected hard with his chin and sent him reeling back as the circle of inmates tightened around them.

Isidrio raised his blade and charged.

Through a fog, Jesus saw the man rushing forward and stepped aside, tripping over punch-drunk legs and falling to the ground.

Isidrio slammed into the prison wall, turned and dove on the downed opponent.

A struggle ensued. They rolled several times along the dirt, the crowd stepping aside and regrouping as the need arose.

Isidrio slammed Jesus's knife-wielding hand into the dirt and the weapon dislodged and clattered along the ground. He slashed at Jesus's neck. Jesus instinctively brought up a right arm and diverted the blade, causing it to slash a large gash across his stomach. With strength rapidly draining, he heaved and rolled as the blade descended and penetrated the dirt inches from his throat.

He crawled along on all fours toward his shank.

Isidrio, his cowboy shirt saturated with blood, crawled after him, grasping Jesus's leg and tugging. Isidrio's strength was draining from the two stab wounds. Jesus glanced back, kicking Isidrio in the head before reaching his knife.

Releasing his grip on Jesus's leg, Isidrio grunted, trying to get up.

But Jesus swung his foot a second time and connected with Isidrio's head, dropping him on all fours. Jesus stood up, stepped forward and kicked again. But Isidrio swept his feet from under him and Jesus crashed to the ground.

Both men slowly stood and faced each other.

Knife outstretched, Isidro charged forward, carving a twelve-inch gash across Jesus's chest. Jesus slumped and Isidrio kicked him hard in the head. Jesus dropped to the ground, clinging to the shank.

Isidrio dove on Jesus.

Jesus wrapped both hands around his blade, thrusting it upward. It pierced through Isidrio's Adam's apple and tore through the back of his neck. Isidrio gurgled, coughed a mouthful of blood into Jesus's face and slumped onto his chest.

Jesus grunted, slid the knife from Isidrio's throat, pushed him aside and crawled away.

Isidro crawled after him, stabbing him in the back. Jesus continued crawling for six feet until he collapsed on his stomach.

Isidrio rolled onto his back, clutching his throat with both hands, gurgling as blood spurted from his mouth and fatal neck wound. He spit a mouthful of blood, looking around, scowling at the group who had instigated the attack. "You ... will all die."

Casting a sideways glance at Jesus, who was stretched face-first in the dirt, barely moving, Isidrio said, "If he's not already dead, that son of a whore will be the first to die."

Isidrio coughed two mouthfuls of blood, twitched for a split-second and died, his vacant black eyes staring up into the blue sky and hot afternoon sun.

Jesus reached a hand behind his back and removed the embedded blade. He rolled over onto his back. He positioned both knives in the shape of a cross over his chest, looked up at the bright yellow sunshine and sighed, the life and death struggle finally over.

Yellow faded to red, red faded to orange, orange faded to gray and gray faded to black.

Chapter Twenty

The small town of Guadalupe y Calvo was shrouded in blackness by the time El Toro, Angelique and Matt arrived. El Toro had arrived punctually at nine that morning to begin the journey, which had taken them over irrefutably bad switchback mountain roads, through small villages and along beautiful forested sections surrounded by majestic mountains and picturesque canyon vistas. They passed cascading waterfalls, life-giving rivers and life-taking military checkpoints and armed bandits along the way.

They had cleared the human and vehicular barriers with relative ease, with the exception of one man-made impasse along a pot-holed and treacherous slice of road in the middle of nowhere. Two pickup trucks and four armed, shady-looking characters had blocked the road, protecting a nearby marijuana crop that was being harvested. They weren't laying out the red-carpet treatment for the guests.

"What brings you up to this area?" a man said, training an AK-47 at El Toro while the other guns were aimed at Angelique and Matt.

And it had been El Toro's vitriolic response that almost got them gunned down Bonnie-and-Clyde style.

"Don't be pointing that gun at me," El Toro said gruffly, drawing a handgun swiftly, cocking the hammer and leveling it at the man's head.

There was a tense Mexican stand-off lasting about thirty seconds—to Matt, the longest thirty seconds of his life—before the firearms were finally lowered. El Toro had a short, clipped conversation with the sinister man pointing a gun at his head. They learned they had some mutual acquaintances, if not friends, in the area. In the Sierra Madre, your survival often came down to who you knew and how powerful they were.

A scene that could have easily erupted into bloodshed and death rapidly turned calm. Tones changed, jokes were exchanged, laughter followed and the men backed up their pickup trucks and cheerfully waved them through.

In that moment, so close to death, in spite of the painful revelations about Angelique's true character, Matt had never felt so alive in his entire life.

But that moment was long gone now as they rolled along a dimly lit side street, drinking beer and listening to music.

The SUV stereo belted out a *narcocorrido*, a folk ballad about drug-traffickers, by famous singer Chuy Quintanilla, whose dead body was recently found in a pool of blood lying next to his SUV, at least two bullet holes to the head, murdered execution-style. The late Quintanilla sang the ballad of Tony Tormenta, the leader of the Gulf Cartel killed in a gunfight in 2010:

> *This is the story of Tony Tormenta*
> *This is the story of the one called the Storm*
> *This is the story of Tony Tormenta*
> *The cruelest of the druglords 'twas ever born*
>
> *Nobody crying for Tony Tormenta*
> *He left the world the same way he came in*
> *Nobody crying for Tony Tormenta*

Covered in the blood of his own countrymen

Killers in the countryside
Lock-step with police
Ain't no translation, man, for that kind of beast
They're killing babies in the street
Strike a deal but it just won't keep

Nobody crying for Tony Tormenta
No time for tears once the storm has passed
Nobody crying for Tony Tormenta
The last man he killed this time was his last

El Toro and Angelique sang along to the music and Matt forced a smile and raised his beer as they glanced at him occasionally for approval. Angelique's voice was soft and melodic—in perfect sync with the music. El Toro, on the other hand, sounded raspy and off-key, and reminded Matt strangely of fingernails raking down a chalkboard. They had all consumed their fair share of beer. For El Toro, traveling through the Sierra Madre and drinking went hand in hand, quite literally.

He was slurring his lyrics by the time he pulled to a stop in front of the Plaza Hotel and turned off the stereo and ignition. "We're here," he announced with as much glee as if they had just pulled up to a five-star beach-front resort.

Two newer black SUVs were parked outside the utilitarian orange-painted concrete building located in *zona centro*, the center of town. The faint sound of televisions blaring and the odd dark barking punctuated the otherwise still night.

Matt sighed deeply, staring at the forbidding darkness. He was a little buzzed, in unfamiliar and dangerous territory with a woman he no longer trusted—actually, feared. Angelique had engaged in many playful conversations with El Toro, who seemed more enamored by her charm and beauty with every passing mile. One conversation, however, turned deadly. She had ordered a hit on Isidrio. El Toro had picked up the phone, snapped a few words off, hung up, and smiled at Angelique, saying, "It will be done. And we have our own reasons for wanting him dead."

Matt's heart sank as he realized they had arrived in Guadalupe y Calvo, very likely on the heels of an assassination. One dead, and how many would be killed tonight in a town where rivals often fought to the death for control of drug distribution routes? And how quickly would Isidrio's death be traced back to El Toro, and by extension, to Matt and Angelique? Vengeance?

And what to do about Angelique?

After reading the emails, Matt had tossed and turned restlessly for most of the night, trying to think his way out of the polylemma. In the end, he had decided not to do or say anything until he arrived home safely—*if* he arrived home safely. Now was not the time or the place for confrontations or accusations, he kept telling himself. Angelique, a Tarahumara now on home-turf, had morphed into a different person—a conscious-less and ruthless warrior who would tolerate little in the way of disrespect.

But Matt also knew Angelique sensed a distinct shift in his attitude and behavior. At the beginning of the trip, he was distant and standoffish, offering little in the way of conversation unless he was asked a question. A few times she had asked what was wrong. Matt had tried his best to smile, saying everything was fine. But he had noticed a small frown of concern crease her pouty lips. And Matt felt his survival depended on becoming a very good actor—faking his emotions—although one part of him still maintained Angelique would never do anything to physically harm him. *Don't kid yourself. She just ordered a hit.*

Luckily, halfway through the journey the comfortable buzz of alcohol had gone some way to helping Matt become more sociable. His smiles had become less forced and more natural.

Matt thanked El Toro and handed over $1,500; a tip was certainly in order for this fine and educational guided tour. After all, he had made it alive, in large part due to El Toro's connections in the region. He doubted they would have been so fortunate traveling guideless.

El Toro said thanks, turned and kissed Angelique on the cheek, shook Matt's hand firmly and they stepped out of the vehicle, retrieved suitcases from the back and stood at the driver door.

"I'll wait until you get inside before I leave," El Toro said. Then his cell phone rang. He answered it, said, "Okay, very good," and hung up with a slight frown. "Good news is, Isidrio's dead. Bad news is, Gloria's boyfriend Jesus is in the local hospital recovering from knife wounds. Gloria's at his side and may not be able to see you until tomorrow."

"Thanks," Angelique said, maintaining her composure.

The sidewalk moved under Matt's feet as he realized the destabilizing effects of the alcohol buzz. Angelique steadied him with an arm as they walked. They stopped at the entrance door to the hotel, waved goodbye to El Toro and entered.

******

Fifteen minutes later, they unpacked some things in a third-floor Spartan-furnished room with metal bars on two small windows overlooking the street. There were two double beds, two wooden armchairs and a small desk equipped with hotel stationery and a wooden chair.

A lone painting of the Virgin of Guadalupe hung crookedly on the whitewashed wall. Her hands were folded in prayer, her eyes barely open, expression calm.

Matt examined the painting, wondering if the iconic image would give him strength as it had Mexican warriors during Mexico's battle for independence in the eighteenth century.

Angelique placed a call to Gloria that went to voicemail. She left a message telling her sister they had arrived and to call as soon as she was free.

"If she's in the hospital, she probably has her cell turned off," Matt said. "You know how it is in hospitals, especially if he's in the intensive-care ward. Cell signals interfere with life-support systems."

She tossed the phone on the bed. "I guess you're right. We'll probably have to wait until tomorrow."

There was a moment of silence before she asked: "Is something wrong with you?"

Yes, there's something very wrong with me. We're stuck in a lawless and dangerous place, you've just had a known Mafioso murdered, and you seem perfectly fine with it. We're running from a murder investigation. And you tell me you love me but you're still chasing and responding to every Tom, Dick and Harry on internet dating sites, even though you call me boyfriend. "No, I'm fine."

"Are you sure?"

Matt nodded.

Angelique tossed her jacket on a nearby chair, grabbed her Blackberry and walked into the bathroom, typing something into the phone.

Maybe it was the alcohol, some new-found bravado, or heartache and grief that had manifested itself in anger. Matt didn't know why he blurted it out. "Are you checking Cupid, Angel? Why don't you see how John Altec is doing? I'm sure he misses you."

******

Angelique froze for a second, dropped the phone into the sink, spun around, and returned. Matt was sitting on the bed. "What are you talking about?" she asked.

"John Altec."

"Who is John Altec?"

"Oh come on, Angel. You can cut the bullshit now. You've told enough lies already."

She sat down on the bed across from Matt. "What are you talking about?"

"I have a lawyer friend who has warned me about you ever since we met. Without my permission he set up a fake profile and started emailing you on Cupid. Needless to say, you responded rather quickly and amorously."

"Oh, that," Angelique said dismissively. "That's nothing. I just responded to be courteous and polite."

"Courteous?" Matt felt the familiar vein bulge and snake across his forehead. "Is sending kisses to someone you just met on a dating site courteous? I have a copy of the chat. Is telling them their photo is nice, that you want to meet them, that you don't have a boyfriend, just being courteous? Excuse me, but I think I'm forgetting the definition of the word courteous. I'll have to look it up again one day."

Now it was Angelique whose black eyes narrowed and brow furrowed. "That's not fair. You set me up with that fake profile. I hate entrapment."

"I didn't have anything to do with it." Matt was about to use Sal's name but caught himself. "But my friend was right. How many other guys have you got on the line on Cupid or whatever other sites you're using, setting up meetings, sending them kisses, telling them you don't have a boyfriend?"

"I don't have anyone—just you. Would you like my password to check my communications?"

"I don't want your password."

"I only started using it about a week ago, because I met a friend who wanted me to teach him English. I've been helping him—that's all."

"You're just piling up lie on top of lie. My friend said you've been using Cupid ever since you met me. I've seen you online on Plenty of Fish after we supposedly became an item."

"Please, I just use Cupid for friends. If you check my profile, you'll see I'm only looking for friends and pen pals."

"Yeah, but your profile also says you're single. What do you think those sites are for? It's a dating site, but I suppose you know that already. And your Facebook profile says you're single too, by the way. Three hundred and sixty-five friends, eh? How many of them are actually your friends, and how many are lovers?"

Angelique kneeled down in front of Matt and looked up at him sorrowfully. She folded her hands in prayer. "I'm just a mere mortal. I'm not perfect. But I love you so much I can't live without you. I'm looking for no other man ..."

"Enough, already. What do you take me for, anyway? An idiot? All you've done is play with my emotions." He got up, stormed into the bathroom and slammed the door. He could hear Angelique talking on the other side, and could still make out her words.

"I want to tell you to believe in me, but I know you don't anymore. I'm out of ideas ... don't know what to say ..."

Matt heard her slump on the bed and a sobbing sound interrupted the monologue for a moment. Then it started again.

"I never toyed with you because if you play that game with me it's messing with my life. I don't want to live without you, so this hurts me. I will not apologize because I haven't done anything wrong. In my life I've had many opportunities, still have many male friends, but since I knew you existed all I want is you. I could not and would not have cheated."

"You were pretty quick to sleep with Alex Liberty after you dumped me," Matt said from behind the door. "Now look at the mess we're in over that."

"Please, Matt. God knows I speak the truth. I'll never fool you. I only have bad luck. God is punishing me. I'm going to die. I'm not bad, I always loved you. I've never felt like this as

I felt for you. I know you don't believe me and think I'm a liar. I'm not the best person, but if I love you a lot and, if there is a God, please let that love live between the two of us."

"You have a twisted perception of love," Matt said from his perch on the toilet. It hadn't been the first time he had sought solace in the earpiece of the great white telephone.

"Maybe God doesn't exist or is punishing me because I'm losing hope—one disaster after another," Angelique said.

"Maybe we can be friends when we get out of here."

"I don't want your friendship. I need your love … if I don't have that, I don't need to live. That's my whole life—suffering, mourning. I swore that this wouldn't happen and it's happening again."

"You brought it on yourself."

"You're just looking at the ugly side of this. You're not counting all the hours I've waited by the phone for your call, checked my email looking for your messages. Maybe you're not so smart, and I can only say love does not exist. It's a drug that has been invented by God to torture humanity. Now you're the instrument of that torture. You hurt me, you take my life. I'll no longer believe in anything. Leave me to cry, suffer and mourn. And die. Goodbye. I love you."

Matt was slumped over, head in hands, when he heard the hotel suite door open and slam shut. He listened to the patter of footsteps fading down the hallway and waited another three minutes before he rose and left the bathroom.

Even though he worried that she might make good on her suicide threat, he was not of a mind to follow her, particularly at night in Guadalupe y Calvo. Instead, he approached the window, slid aside the sheer fabric blinds and peered down the dark street. Nothing. *Fuck. Why did I open my big mouth? She could have me killed and no one would ever know.*

Chapter Twenty-One

Should I kill myself? Should I? No, better see Gloria before I do anything like that. Storming out of the hotel, Angelique had been so upset she actually contemplated jumping in front of a black SUV that had sped past. But walking for five minutes—a torrent of emotion coursing through her body and mind—had finally given way to the voice of reason. Thoughts of Gloria dissipated her anger and grief. Before she made any further decisions, she wanted to reunite with Gloria and meet Jesus, her heroic boyfriend who had ended the life of Isidrio, the man who had killed her parents. *I need to thank Jesus.*

She buttoned up her black jacket—the night was getting chilly and windy—and felt in her pocket for the cell phone. She sighed, feeling its familiar shape. *Thank God. I might need it.*

Calmer, she retraced the events in her mind, trying to decide if she had done anything wrong. *I wouldn't have done anything with John. I just needed to know that other people love me. I need reassurance that I'm attractive from many sources. What's so wrong with that? Everything. You don't trust or like yourself enough to love Matt, don't trust him enough to love you like you need to be loved. You're repeating the same old patterns, girl. You did that with your ex-husband. That's no good ... I should apologize.*

Having no idea where she was going, she walked past a dark alley and suddenly heard a tinny, rattling sound. She jumped and a voice echoed from the darkness. "Give me some money."

She stopped, strained her eyes, and saw the dark silhouette of a figure weaving back and forth, approaching. "I need a drink. Give me some money."

She stopped, watching the man stagger forward. A grizzled head with a mop of dark disheveled hair appeared out of the obscurity, illuminated faintly by a glowing streetlight. She watched the drunken spectacle. As he neared, Angelique saw he had lines creasing a pudgy face, a thick beard, halfway unbuttoned cowboy shirt, a bulbous beer belly, urine-stained blue jeans and cowboy boots. "I want some money. I need a drink."

Angelique's first instinct had been to run, but she quickly thought better of showing fear. This was her first night in what should have been her stomping grounds growing up, and she wasn't about to start by acting like a coward. *No. You do that and people walk all over you. I don't have the constitution for that.*

"Did you ever hear the word 'please'? Or are you the kind of person who goes around demanding things all the time?" she asked in perfect Spanish.

The drunkard took a step forward but then staggered three sideways steps before the wall of a building stopped his momentum. He steadied himself with two hands on the wall and sized up Angelique, his head slowly lolling from side to side. He was silent for a moment.

He couldn't hurt a fly. "Haven't you had enough to drink?" Angelique asked.

"Please can I have some money for a drink?"

"That's better. You're saying please now. Tell you what. You point me toward the General Hospital and I'll give you some money."

"Who the fuck are you?" the man snapped, suddenly lurching forward.

Angelique easily sidestepped the unsteady charge.

The man tripped on the curb and fell face-first on the road, moaning in pain.

"See what you get when you talk nasty?" Angelique said.

He rolled over on his back, staring up at her. "Help me up?"

"Where's the hospital?"

He scratched a bleeding forehead and pointed down the street. "That way?"

"How far?"

"Walking ... twenty minutes, maybe. By car, two minutes, I guess."

"Are you sure?"

"I need a drink."

"Are you sure it's that way?"

"Straight down about five blocks and then turn right, almost at the end of the road."

She helped him to his feet, careful not to touch the urine-stained jeans. He stared at her. "You're beautiful."

She handed him two hundred pesos. "You're drunk."

"Even if I wasn't, I'd say you're beautiful."

"Take care of yourself," she said, turning and walking away.

"Wait," he said. "Who are you? You look familiar."

"Mind your manners. You can say thank you."

She heard shuffling of footsteps behind her and realized he was attempting to follow.

"Thank you," he shouted.

She glanced behind, saw him collide with a metal garbage can and wipe out on the sidewalk, the garbage can clanging along in front of his outstretched body, emptying debris.

A few dogs barked and some house lights illuminated. She checked her watch: 8:47 pm. Not too late to see Gloria, with any luck.

She continued down the dark street. Receiving directions from three more people, including a nervous-looking shopkeeper in a small convenience store, she could finally see the lights of the small hospital in the distance, about a hundred yards away. She pulled out her phone, checking to see if Matt had called, and noticed a text message from him: *Where are you? Don't do anything stupid, please.*

She sighed. *He still cares about me.* She typed *I love you,* clicked send, and entered the hospital. A nurse scowled as she approached an administration station, waved an index finger and pointed to the phone. "Turn that off. And visiting hours are over."

Doors burst open and two medical staff, accompanied by a sobbing young woman, wheeled a stretcher past her. The bullet-riddled victim moaned and clutched his blood-soaked chest. Angelique watched them disappear down the hall, turned the phone off and addressed the nurse. "I'm looking for Jesus."

"Are you family?"

"Gloria Alvarez is my sister, his girlfriend."

The woman's features softened. "Gloria Alvarez?"

"Yes, is she here?"

"You look a lot like your sister. Are you twins?"

"She's a year younger."

"Gloria's a very honest and hardworking woman. She's well-liked around here. And so happy—in spite of her struggles. I've never met someone with such a peaceful demeanor. I hope you're like Gloria."

"Very much so," Angelique said, offering her most naively innocent smile.

"Jesus is on the third floor. Room 304. Gloria's by his side. Please don't stay too long." She pointed down the hall to a door leading to a stairwell.

Angelique thanked her and continued on, her heart pounding with anticipation. She reached the third floor and walked down the long corridor. The moaning and groaning of patients punctuated the silence. The smell of urine, vomit and disinfectant assaulted her nostrils and she scrunched her nose. And there was something else—the acrid, coppery smell of blood.

An armed guard outside the room patted her down, smiling and apologizing as he touched her twice inappropriately. Angelique fought an urge to knee him in the nuts, but an afterthought prevented the punishment. He was likely one of El Toro's men charged with protecting Jesus. She didn't want to injure Jesus's protector, and by extension her protector, not to mention Gloria or Matt.

The man opened the door and Angelique entered. Gloria sat on a chair beside the bed, holding Jesus's hand and gazing into his eyes. Jesus had two IV drips, one containing blood. His neck, chest and stomach were bandaged, his eye sockets swollen black. He smiled weakly at Angelique.

Gloria spun around and ran into her sister's arms. "You're here," Angelique said. "Thank God I've finally found my sister."

They embraced tightly. Angelique pulled back to look at her sister. They both wiped tears from their eyes.

Angelique felt like she was looking at herself in the mirror. She couldn't believe the striking resemblance. Gloria was a little shorter in height and a little thinner, with smaller breasts and buttocks. Gloria also bore a two-inch scar on her left temple, the result of refusing the advances of a drunken patron at the cantina. The patron had smashed a beer bottle over her head and, once El Toro found out, had paid for it with a chest full of lead.

Otherwise, they were almost an identical match. They even wore their long black hair parted down the middle the same way.

"I can't believe it," Angelique said. "My sister. Finally, my sister. We look so much alike."

Beaming, Gloria nodded. A silence followed and Gloria finally pointed to Jesus, who was staring up at them from the bed curiously. "This is Jesus. He's had a little accident. I'll tell you about it later."

Angelique approached the bed. She was about to thank Jesus, but then a thought occurred to her. *Gloria doesn't know I ordered the hit.* El Toro had indicated during the earlier conversation that Jesus would be fully apprised, but Jesus must not have told Gloria that Angelique was involved. Jesus had yet to meet Angelique, and already he was protecting her honor, withholding information from Gloria that could potentially harm the newly formed family bond. After all, Angelique's orders had almost cost this brave young man his life.

Angelique gently touched Jesus's arm and kissed him on the cheek. "Nice to meet you."

"A pleasure. You look so much like Gloria."

Gloria put an arm around her sister's shoulder. "We have so much to get caught up on. Where's Matt?"

"He's at the hotel. He was tired, but he'll be here tomorrow."

They sat down beside Jesus's bed.

"Do you know about Isidrio?" Jesus asked Angelique.

A frown creased Gloria's features.

"El Toro told us when we arrived," Angelique said. She looked at Gloria concernedly and took her hand before continuing: "El Toro told me to apologize to you for spilling it, but he also told me that our parents were murdered many years ago, and that Isidrio was one of the men responsible. I understand why you wanted to tell me in person."

Gloria wiped away a tear. "It doesn't matter now. It would have been hard for me to tell you."

"But Isidrio's dead now," Jesus said. "His killing days are over. I've avenged the death of your parents."

Angelique put a hand on his arm. "I want to thank you for that. You're a very brave man. You could have gotten yourself killed."

"It's how things get done around here," Jesus said. "It's the law of the Sierra Madre. But I'm out of prison now and won't be going back. El Toro's group will protect me."

"I hope so," Gloria said, worry creasing her brow. "I want to be with you always."

Jesus smiled. "We will be. I promise."

Chapter Twenty-Two

Matt had promised himself he wouldn't leave the hotel at night in unfamiliar and dangerous surroundings. But, other than the *I love you* text message, he hadn't heard from Angelique in over two hours. His mind envisioned worst-case scenarios—she had typed the message just before killing herself. Now, she was lying somewhere, wrists slashed, in a pool of her own blood. But surely she would want to meet Jesus and Gloria? Maybe she was at the hospital? Or maybe she had been attacked and kidnapped, raped or murdered?

He had already sent three text messages and three voice messages. Had she turned her phone off prior to killing herself? Had the kidnappers destroyed it? Wait a minute. If she was at the hospital, she would have to turn the phone off.

It seemed like the most likely scenario. But, considering where he was, it brought small comfort to his troubled and inebriated mind. Thanks to a friendly clerk at the hotel lobby desk, he was drinking beer in the hotel suite. An hour ago, he had ventured downstairs and managed a peek down dark streets, before the clerk motioned him inside with a cautionary wave of his index finger. "You don't want to walk around at night. You're a gringo and you don't know anyone here."

"Is there a liquor store nearby?" Matt had asked in passable Spanish.

"Three blocks straight down," the clerk said. "But it's dangerous to go out right now, especially for you."

After a short conversation about Angelique—the clerk had not seen her leave—the short bald man had wandered into the back room and returned with a twelve-pack of Tecate, which he sold to Matt. Matt had tipped him generously and returned to the room, where he planned on drowning his sorrows in beer.

And four beers later, he was accomplishing his goal. He reached for a fifth beer from the bathroom sink filled with cold water and paced the room, his mind a jumble of thoughts. What was foremost on his mind was Angelique's safety. And, if she returned, whether he should forgive her. *Isn't love all about forgiveness? Didn't she tell me that? Maybe, but she doesn't even think she's done anything wrong. How do you forgive someone like that?*

He absently approached the window, pulled the blinds aside and gazed outside. A newer, dark-colored SUV pulled in front of the hotel and parked on the narrow street. Two men armed with automatic assault rifles exited and went inside the hotel. It was the second SUV Matt had seen arrive in the last hour. Now there were four parked outside. *The troops are coming in. For what?*

He continued pacing, drinking and thinking. *Why should I forgive her?* He stared up at the image of the Virgin of Guadalupe and a light bulb inside his head clicked on. *She's talked of suicide before, sounded very serious.*

And there was more—the conversation on the plane, just prior to the excellent oral care. Angelique's mood had suddenly darkened and she had a hard time holding back tears as she relayed her story of being kidnapped at the tender age of five, taken to San Agustinillo and repeatedly raped, verbally abused and beaten by a man she thought was her father. If that wasn't enough, she was at Edgardo's beck and call 24/7, a life reduced practically to slave labor. No wonder she couldn't love anyone, or felt the need to seek love from multiple men. The way she had been treated was much worse than abandonment by a father figure. Edgardo had viciously abused the privilege.

Not to mention the machismo Mexican men who had used and degraded her. Wasn't there a rape or two included in the history of those exes? Matt thought so, but Angelique had relayed her life story with such passion, heartache and sobs he had trouble remembering all the details. By the end of it, she was sobbing on the plane quietly, her head pressed tight against his chest, trying to conceal the emotion from other passengers.

Where's your understanding, Matt? Forgive her and move on. No one's perfect, least of all yourself.

He made up his mind. He was going to find Angelique. He grabbed a jacket, drained his fifth beer, put one in each side pocket, locked the suite and headed out.

While grudgingly drawing a map of the hospital's location, the hotel desk clerk eyed him wearily and offered the same shaking index finger.

As the clerk drew the map, an AK-47-armed man wearing military fatigues and polished black military boots entered the hotel, eyed Matt cautiously, smiled to the clerk and went down the hall to his room.

The clerk handed the completed map to Matt and offered a last warning. "You're crazy to go out at this time of the night."

"My girlfriend's missing, and I'm going to find her," he said as he spun around and walked into the obscurity of the night.

Two blocks later, he came across a tipped-over steel garbage can on the side of the road, litter strewn along its path. A man was stretched out beside it. Judging by the awkward way his body was positioned, it appeared as if someone had dragged him out of the path of oncoming traffic.

Matt stopped abruptly, initially thinking the man was dead. Then the man hiccupped, burped and snored loudly. Studying him, Matt took a few breaths, trying to force his speeding heart rate to decelerate.

Then it happened.

A rustling sound in the alley—a dark figure moving swiftly toward him. Matt froze and his eyes widened as he realized—a little too late—what was happening. The man grabbed him by the jacket collar with one hand and pushed the jagged edge of a broken beer bottle to his throat. "Give me your money."

Maybe it was the alcohol, or perhaps the fear, but it certainly wasn't due to lack of experience that Matt resisted. He had heard the stories. If someone tries to rob you, don't resist. Give them your money; your life is worth more than a hundred dollars. Better still, carry a wad of "robber's cash" around with fake bills on the inside of the wad, smaller bills on the outside, making it look like a small fortune. Give the robber the robber's cash and keep your spending money hidden in a concealed pocket, a money belt, somewhere the robber isn't likely to look. Chances are, the robber will be in a hurry, perhaps just as nervous as you, take the money and run, only to discover later he was duped by a seasoned traveler.

But Matt didn't have any robber's cash. Even if he did, he probably wouldn't have thought to use it. It had happened so fast. Matt stepped back, sweeping a forearm up and striking the broken beer bottle, not quite hard enough to dislodge it.

The man stepped back, angry. "You don't want to give me your money? Then I'll take it from you. And I'll take more than that."

He threw a punch that connected with a thwack to the side of Matt's head. Vision clouding, he staggered back and dropped to the pavement as his legs disobeyed brain commands.

The passed-out drunk man snored loudly.

The assailant quickly mounted Matt and thrust the jagged edge of glass to his throat. Matt turned his head at the last second and heard glass shattering on concrete. He extracted a full can of beer from a pocket and swung it wildly at the attacker.

The beer can connected with a popping sound as it struck the man's head, dented and exploded, foam gushing like a mini fountain.

The sleeping drunk opened his eyes. "I need a drink." He closed them again and resumed a nasally snore.

The attacker was hardly fazed by the beer-can blow. He wiped dripping foam from his face and plunged the jagged edge down a second time.

Matt saw it nearing and knew he wouldn't be able to move fast enough. It was too close, the man was too strong, and Matt was too drunk and too dizzy from the blow to the head.

"Noooooooooooo," Matt shouted, at the same time thinking how ridiculous his last words sounded.

Kaplow ... kaplow!

The hand with the jagged edge wavered, slamming what remained of the bottle hard into the road, shattering it into smithereens. His head slumped onto Matt's chest. Matt realized the ringing in his ears was from the deafening sound of gunshot blasts. He turned his head sideways and saw a woman in a black dress leveling a smoking gun at him. He brought a forearm to his eyes. "No, no, no."

But, after a few seconds, he found the courage to peer through the forearm shield. "Angelique? You saved my life."

The woman tucked the gun into an ankle holster. "I'm Gloria."

With Gloria's help, Matt slid the dead man off him. Out of the darkness, Angelique appeared and helped him to his feet. Matt's black jacket was soaked in the dead man's blood.

"Are you okay?" Angelique asked. "What happened to your head?"

A goose egg was growing out of the left side of Matt's head. It was scratched and reddish-blue.

Matt's heart was still racing. "I think so. He punched me."

"Matt, Gloria, Gloria, Matt," Angelique said.

Still a little dazed, Matt hugged Gloria and kissed the air beside her cheek. He couldn't believe how much she resembled Angelique. "Nice to meet you. And thanks."

"Don't worry," Gloria said, pointing to the corpse and tearing up. "Manolito tried to rape me once. He's scum. And I didn't have a choice."

"No, you didn't," Matt said.

Angelique turned to Matt. "What were you doing out here?"

"Looking for you."

"That's so sweet," Angelique said. "I'm so sorry about earlier." Angelique hugged him tightly and they kissed. "I know I did wrong and I hope you forgive me."

Matt stared at her blankly. At that moment he wanted more than anything else to forget Angelique's indiscretion. But ultimately he didn't know if he could. He nodded.

The passed-out drunk man sound-tracked the embrace with another loud, nasally snore.

"We need to go," Gloria said. Her soft features had turned serious as she stared at the corpse on the road. "I've never killed anyone before."

"Let's drag him into the alley," Angelique said. "And get out of here."

They dragged the body into the alley, hiding him behind some debris, and exited the alley together.

Matt looked at the drunk, still snoring. "What about him?"

"That's Ruiz," Gloria said. "The town drunk—or one of them. He's always sleeping in the streets. He's probably seen more people get killed than anyone here. He won't remember anything. And besides, he's out."

"Don't worry about him," Angelique said. "Let's get out of here."

Matt glanced back at snoring Ruiz as they turned and hurried back to the hotel. "We're in a lot of shit."

There was an unsettling silence before Gloria responded. "No were not. We've got El Toro. And El Toro never liked Manolito for attempting to violate me. Manolito's days were numbered, anyway. Besides, Manolito's murder won't really be investigated by police. There's nothing in it for them. They're far too busy to worry about a low-life like him. We just need to get you cleaned up."

Matt remembered his other beer. He pulled it out and cracked it open. He thought it would go some way to calming his frayed nerves. It couldn't hurt.

He offered it to Gloria first. Her earlier calm expression had given way to a case of the jitters. She glanced around nervously as they walked.

"Thank you," she said, taking the can and sipping before offering it to Angelique.

"Don't mind if I do," Angelique said calmly, gulping a few mouthfuls before handing it to Matt.

Outside the hotel, Gloria said goodbye, promising to meet them tomorrow afternoon at the hospital, where she planned an all-night vigil. She explained she had planned on returning that night but killing Manolito had stressed and fatigued her. She needed some time alone to calm her nerves.

"Thanks so much for saving my life," Matt said, releasing her from a hug. "I owe you big-time. If you ever need anything, don't hesitate to call."

"I'm not the kind of person to take you up on the offer, but thanks," Gloria said. She turned and walked down the street.

They watched her disappear around a corner before entering the hotel. To shield his blood-soaked jacket from the desk clerk, Matt shadowed Angelique.

But the clerk, evidently noticing the bruising and lump on Matt's head, raised the cautionary finger again. "I told you and you didn't listen."

******

While Matt showered, Angelique disappeared with the soiled evidence, dumped it into a storm drain and returned to the room with a bucket of ice.

Matt heard the door close just as he stepped out of the shower. "Angelique, is that you?"

"Yes. I got rid of the evidence."

"Good." He towel-dried his hair, put on a t-shirt and pair of multi-pocketed travel pants, and sat on the bed.

Angelique sat on the opposite bed, facing him. "I really hope you can forgive me. I understand I did something wrong. I don't want to make excuses, but I don't think I would have done anything. But I'm sorry. So sorry."

Still a little shell-shocked from the recent murder of his would-be robber, Matt didn't have the energy for any more drama. "I'd like to believe you. I'd like to forgive you. I just need some time." He rubbed his injured head.

Angelique went into the bathroom, returned with a small towel, wrapped it in ice, and handed it to him. "Here, you need to ice that."

Matt took the folded towel and pressed it to the goose egg. He was mentally and emotionally spent. "Honey, could you grab me a beer from the bathroom sink please? And put some ice in there if you don't mind."

She put some ice into the bathroom sink and returned with two beers. She handed one to Matt, popped the top of hers and raised it. "Cheers to a new union with no more lies."

Matt opened his beer, toasted, and they drank.

Angelique's phone rang. She looked at the number and smiled at Matt before answering. "Hi Victor. How are you? Yes, he's here, hang on."

"Who's that?"

"Don't worry, I put him on hold. It's my friend from Mexico. We grew up together and he lives in Vancouver now. Matt, I'm sorry if you don't like what I've done, but I called Victor from the hospital after visiting Gloria and Jesus. I told him to talk to you and vouch for my character."

"Is he your boyfriend?"

"No, you're my boyfriend, I hope. He and I were childhood sweethearts, but that was a long time ago. We're just close friends now. You must be thinking, 'Why doesn't this woman have any friends?' But, I do. And I want you to talk to one of them. He'll vouch for me. He knows how much I love you."

Matt was getting confused. While he was impressed that Angelique would go to such great lengths to prove her worthiness, there was a pang of jealousy knotting an already-upset stomach. *Just get it over with*, he thought. "Okay, give me the phone."

She pressed a button on the phone and handed it over.

After the cursory greetings, Matt asked, "You're a friend of Angelique's?"

"I've known her for ten years."

"Oh."

"Maybe I shouldn't intervene, but my friend Angelique is very sad. I know she has a big heart. And if she says she loves you, she loves you. She explained things to me and told me you feel betrayed."

"Betrayed is an understatement."

"I'm very fond of Angelique and I don't want her to suffer. Believe me, she loves you very much. She's very respectful, an exceptional person and a very good woman."

"I think I can be the judge of that."

"Forgive me if I've done something wrong, but I think it's better to love and carry resentment than to have no love at all; especially a love as strong as Angelique's. Believe me—I didn't want to get involved. But I couldn't bear Angelique's crying on the phone and became very worried for her emotional state. Please understand, Angelique would die without your love."

"Sometimes I think I know her and sometimes I think I don't know her at all. I don't know what she'd do."

"Believe me when I tell you she loves you like crazy. I am alone and I so crave a woman to love me with the depth of love such as Angelique's. That kind of love is very difficult to find. A woman like Angelique is very difficult to find."

"I'd agree with that."

"Forgive me again for intervening, but you have the opportunity of a lifetime sitting in the room with you right now. I hope you can find it in your heart to forgive her and make it work. I'm going to go now. I've probably overstepped my boundaries. Enjoy your stay in the Sierra Madre. I hope one day to meet you. Bye, Matt."

The line went dead and Matt looked up at Angelique's sorrowful eyes. Either she was a master manipulator and a master of disguise, or this enigmatic woman really loved him. He looked down at the tent growing in his travel pants. It never failed. Whenever he heard—or read—the word love in conjunction with Angelique, he became aroused.

Angelique noticed the protrusion and grinned mischievously, undoing a couple of buttons on her blouse. She moved in close, kissed his cheek and expertly glided her hand along his leg toward his throbbing member.

Matt felt a tingling sensation and a soft moan escaped his lips.

He might be in hell, but he was in heaven.

Chapter Twenty-Three

"If I die, I'll go to heaven," Jesus said.

"You're not going to die," Gloria said, holding Jesus's hand as she sat at his bedside the following sun-lit afternoon. "Don't talk like that."

"I'm just saying, we're all going to die sometime. We may as well come to grips with it."

"You're going to recover and we're getting married."

"Okay." He smiled. "I'd like that very much."

Angelique and Matt sat bedside, listening to their conversation. They had arrived an hour ago, after meeting Gloria for lunch at a nearby restaurant. Upon entering the hospital, Matt was immediately struck by the nervous gestures and expressions of staff; they were constantly darting their eyes around while furtively going about their duties. There was a pervading vibe of doom and gloom in the utilitarian building, as if they were waiting for something terrible to happen. He had read the stories on the internet of doctors and nurses fleeing hospitals in the past out of fear for their lives.

And, as if to reinforce that point, there were plenty of armed men patrolling hospital corridors. El Toro had beefed up security of Jesus's room. Two armed guards stood at the door, while another guard was stationed in the room, sitting on a chair by a window, his alert eyes focused on the parking lot below.

Matt had said little to Jesus after introductions were made, other than to thank him and wish him a speedy recovery. Immediately after he thanked Jesus, he felt stupid. *I'm thanking him for killing somebody and putting our lives in danger.* But he couldn't help but be impressed by Jesus's calm bravado and willingness to accept and even embrace death. The man was fearless. It reminded Matt of the song by the late Lou Reed, *Fly Into the Sun.*

> *I would not run from the holocaust*
> *I would not run from the bomb*
> *I'd welcome the chance to meet my maker*
> *and fly into the sun*

He thought of his near-death experience last night and realized in many ways he wasn't half the man Jesus was. Matt had been petrified, damn close to pissing his pants and blubbering like an idiot—far from the calm and accepting demeanor exuded by the slashed-up and injured man in front of him.

Jesus's brand of justice called for immediate retribution for honor besmirched or perceived injustice, while Matt fretted, worried and relied on the Canadian legal system and the expertise of lawyers. *We're worlds apart, but who's right and who's wrong?*

"Are you okay?" Angelique asked, squeezing Matt's hand and smiling. "You look nervous."

It disrupted Matt's train of thought. But it didn't matter. He didn't have the answers, probably never would. "I'm fine."

"Do you forgive me?" Angelique whispered, while Jesus and Gloria talked.

She's made mistakes—and she'll probably continue to make mistakes, Matt thought. *Everyone makes mistakes. But look at those eyes. She loves you. And last night—wow. Have you ever made love with a woman as pleasing and passionate as her? It gets better every time.* Matt smiled, leaned over, kissed Angelique and whispered, "We'll talk later, honey." He noticed Gloria leaning over and kissing Jesus at exactly the same time.

"Can you get me some water?" Jesus asked Gloria. His nurse had called in sick today and there wouldn't be a replacement. "I'm thirsty."

"Sure," Gloria said.

"I'll get it," Angelique said, standing up. "You carry on."

Gloria was about to protest, but Angelique was already halfway to the door.

"Get down," the guard at the window suddenly shouted.

A burst of machine-gun fire erupted from the parking lot and shards of window glass and bullets sprayed into the room.

The guard trained his machine gun out the window and returned fire.

Pandemonium, panic and chaos erupted. To the deafening sound of staccato-bursts of machine-gun fire, shouts and screams echoed eerily through the hallways as people ran for their lives.

Matt dove to the floor along with Gloria. Jesus ripped the IVs from his wrist, got up, and walked calmly to the door as two guards entered and ran to the window, firing.

"Give me a gun," Jesus demanded. "I'm not going down without a fight."

A third guard appeared at the door and handed him an AK-47.

Jesus turned to Gloria and Matt. "Get out of here. Now!" Then Jesus went to the window and began firing.

Matt grabbed Gloria's arm and they crawled along the floor toward the door as Jesus and El Toro's men provided cover-fire.

Suddenly Matt gasped. He saw Angelique sprawled on the floor on her back in a pool of her own blood. She had been shot by two bullets—one in the chest, the other in the neck. She held one hand to her neck as blood spurted between her fingers and snaked down her chest.

"Angel," Matt said, crawling over, clasping her free hand and leaning in close.

"Oh my God," Gloria said, reaching her sister and placing a hand on her bleeding neck. "No, not my sister! Please God, not my sister!"

Bullets sprayed, ricocheted and zinged everywhere.

"You're going to be okay," Matt said, watching the life drain from her eyes. "You'll be okay."

Angelique coughed and a mouthful of blood dribbled down her chin. Her breathing had become rapid. "No I'm not."

"Yes you are, Angel. Yes you are," Matt said. "Someone get a doctor! Someone get a fucking doctor over here!"

"Angel, don't die, please don't die," Gloria said, tears streaming down her face.

"It's okay," Angelique said, blood dribbling from her mouth. "I've finally met you. I've waited my whole life and now I know you. I love you."

"I love you, too," Gloria said, resting her head on Angelique's chest.

Angelique's gaze met Matt's. "Kiss me," she said. "Kiss me for the last time. I love you. You're my life."

Matt leaned in closer. "I love you. And I forgive you. I'll always love you." He kissed Angel and slowly lifted his head, her blood smeared across his lips and face. She smiled, winked, breathed her last breath and was still—her black mesmerizing eyes boring into his soul.

"Someone get a fucking doctor," Matt yelled. "Please!"

"Nooooooo," Gloria shouted, hugging Angelique, kissing her cheek. "You can't die."

"Ahhhhhhhhhhhhhh," Jesus moaned, and dropped to the floor in front of the window.

"Fuck sakes," Matt said, seeing him drop.

Gloria screamed and ran to his side, kneeling over.

A V-pattern of bullets was sprayed across his chest. Blood oozed from the wounds. His labored breathing came in short gasps.

Matt crawled over to Jesus and Gloria. Two other guards lay riddled with bullets on the floor below the windows.

Gloria was hysterical. "Nooooo, noooo, nooo ..."

"My love," Jesus said. "Calm, please. We will be united in the afterlife. I promise." Blood dribbled from his mouth and down his chin.

Matt squeezed Jesus's hand while Gloria kissed him repeatedly on the lips and cheeks, saying, "I love you, I love you, I love you ... don't die, baby ... don't die, please. I can't live without you. Don't die ..." She trailed off and broke into soft, whimpering sobs.

She slowly withdrew her face as Jesus's breathing grew more labored. He looked Matt straight in the eye and said: "Promise me you'll take care of her. She has no one now."

"I promise," Matt said, eyes welling with tears.

Jesus closed his eyes, twitched and said, "God, I welcome your embrace." A calmness suffused his features. He twitched once more and was still.

"We have to go. Now!" It was El Toro, standing at the doorway, bullet belts crisscrossed around his chest, an AK-47 pointed at the window. He pointed at the three dead soldiers sprawled out on the floor, pools of blood snaking out around them. "We're outnumbered."

In a fit of rage, Gloria suddenly jumped up, snatched a hand gun off the floor, approached the window and cracked off four shots toward a black SUV. Two of the rival cartel's soldiers dropped dead.

"I'll kill you all," Gloria said, shooting. "I'll kill you all."

El Toro dove for cover.

Matt leaped up and grabbed her arm, ducking as a barrage of bullets blasted inside the room. "Gloria, let's go."

Her eyes were wide, wild and determined. "I'll kill them all."

El Toro got up off the floor, motioning to Matt. "Bring her. Quickly. Let's go."

Matt pulled her arm. She turned around to face him, a flicker of recognition appearing in otherwise faraway eyes.

"Jesus is dead. Angel's dead. We can't bring them back," Matt said.

Gloria ducked down to retrieve an AK-47 and a bullet belt from a dead soldier, and tossed them to Matt. She stripped another soldier of his arsenal and flung it over her shoulder.

El Toro waved them toward the door, spraying cover-fire out the shattered windows.

They ran into the hallway. A few seconds later, El Toro, walking backward and firing, appeared in the hall. He pointed and they sprinted toward an exit sign at the end of the hall.

A man appeared at the other end and started chase, firing a handgun.

Bullets whizzed past their heads and smashed into the wall as they reached the door. Matt opened it while El Toro spun around—*rat a tat tat … rat a tat tat*—and shot and killed the pursuer.

They ran down the stairs, exiting a back door to a waiting red SUV. They climbed in and sped out of the hospital parking lot, two black SUVs in hot pursuit. El Toro, sitting in the shotgun seat, barked out a few orders to the driver, rolled down the window and began firing at the pursuing vehicles.

Gloria, sitting in the backseat alongside Matt, gave him a crash-course on weapons handling.

"Incoming on the right," El Toro shouted and the driver jerked hard left as a rocket-propelled grenade struck a nearby house and exploded with a large boom.

The driver made a series of quick turns before the red SUV exited the small town and barreled down a gradually ascending stretch of road leading into the mountains.

"Incoming left," El Toro shouted. The vehicle veered right and a whizzing grenade struck a tree, exploding with a thundering boom. The tree burst into flames and a ring of black smoke lazily drifted above the inferno. The red SUV shook with the force of the explosion and skidded on the gravel surface for a few seconds before the tires gripped and the vehicle accelerated.

El Toro turned to Matt and Gloria. "Shoot out the fucking window. I need some help."

Matt and Gloria rolled their windows down simultaneously and began firing. Matt blew out the front tire of the first pursing SUV and it spun out, flipped end-over-end twice before bursting into flames and exploding with a boom.

"Nice shot," El Toro said. "We'll make a warrior out of you yet."

But the other SUV was right behind and closing fast.

The road grew steep and winding. The driver expertly fishtailed around the corners. But the black SUV was still gaining, the attacking driver apparently equally as skilled as El Toro's driver.

Matt saw a grenade launcher emerge from the window of the pursuer. "We've got incoming."

The speeding grenade struck the right rear wheel of El Toro's SUV and exploded, sending the vehicle flying into the air, somersaulting. It flew off a small cliff, bounced once before skidding, crunching and grinding to a stop upside down on the steep bank of a cliff.

It took Matt a few seconds to realize what had happened. He opened his eyes, dazed, and felt blood trickling down his nose. Gloria was crumpled up in a fetal position next to him, unconscious. He glanced at the front seat. Both front airbags had burst open on impact, but a tree branch had pierced through the windshield, penetrated the airbag, and sliced right through the driver's neck. The broken branch had also sliced through the front seat and its spear-like tip dangled a few inches from Matt's head, oozing blood and guts. The driver's eyes bulged and blood gushed from the fatal wound.

El Toro twisted and turned in the airbag, unsheathed a knife and sliced it open. Air escaped with a whoosh, and he turned around. "We've got to get out of here. Now!"

Matt smelled gasoline, antifreeze, burning rubber and smoke. And the acrid, coppery scent of blood.

From above, he heard the pursuing SUV skid to a stop, doors open and machine-gun fire erupt.

Shit, Matt thought. *This thing's going to blow.*

El Toro winced. One of his legs was crushed. He was pinned inside the vehicle. He turned to Matt and pointed to Gloria. "Get her out of here."

"What about you?"

"Forget about me. Live by fire. Die by fire. Get the fuck out of here."

As bullets ricocheted off metal, Matt shook Gloria. "Wake up." He noticed a cut on the back of her head that oozed blood into her thick black hair, matting it to her head, back, and white coat. He inched his way along the inside of the smashed-in roof, and crawled out through the open window.

Reaching in, he grabbed Gloria's leg and pulled. Her body inched toward the opening.

A small flame ignited on the hood and snaked its way to the passenger compartment.

"Hurry," El Toro said.

Matt found superhuman strength he never knew he possessed and pulled Gloria from the vehicle.

He took a step back, but found only air. He lost his balance and fell down the brush-filled embankment, dragging Gloria down with him. They rolled about thirty feet down the steep incline before crashing into a thick pile of brush.

Matt raised his head, heard a loud boom, and watched the red SUV explode into a ball of flame. Black smoke twirled up into the heavens and El Toro screamed horribly as he burned to death in a fiery grave.

Four men stood on the shoulder of a hairpin turn at the top of the cliff. They slowly lowered their weapons. Matt could just barely hear the conversation.

"Do you think they're all dead?"

"I think so."

"Don't think so. Be sure."

"I can't go down there. It's too steep."

"If you don't go down there, and Esteban finds out there are survivors, then you're dead."

"Come with me?"

"No, Rufino will go with you. We'll wait here."

Matt watched as the two men slowly scrambled down the treacherous precipice.

"Gloria," he whispered. She lay beside him in the thick brush. He shook her. "Gloria."

Her eyes slowly fluttered open. "Where are ..."

"Shhhh ... we're in danger." Matt pointed to the top of the cliff. They could hear branches snapping as the men scrambled down.

Gloria slowly gathered her extremities, moving each limb individually until she was satisfied. She wiped the back of her head, examined her bloody hand, and frowned. She blinked a few times and gazed around. "I know this area. Follow me."

Matt wiped his bloody face. He found no serious damage to his extremities other than some cuts and bruises. There was a two-inch cut above his right eyebrow, dripping blood into his eye.

He crawled behind Gloria through the thicket of bushes. They arrived at a grassy knoll on the other side. She pointed to an oddly-shaped oak tree about 200 yards in the distance. It grew straight for ten or so feet, then jutted out crookedly to the right, as if lowering a supplicating hand.

"There's a trail there," she whispered. "Let's go."

"Wait. They'll hear us."

They froze, watching through cracks in the bushes as the men neared.

"We can't stay here," Gloria whispered. "They'll kill us."

"Yeah, but if we move they'll hear us and shoot us."

One man lost his footing on some loose rocks, slipped and rolled down the steep incline, screaming in terror as he crashed into the flaming SUV. He stepped away, green military fatigues completely engulfed in flames—a staggering ball of fire. His blood-curdling screams of agony echoed through vast canyons as he rolled on the ground to no avail and died a slow and painful death.

Gloria stared wide-eyed and terrified.

Matt turned his head away momentarily, the horrifying sight creating a wave of nausea. He swallowed a lump of vomit that had inched up his throat and grimaced as the stomach-acid-laced food particles slowly slid down into the pit of his stomach.

The other man stopped and looked up at the top of the cliff, where the two men were watching. "Keep going," one of them yelled.

The drug cartel soldier lay on his back, slid about ten feet, found footing and continued, making sure to give the burning vehicle and the burning flesh a wide berth.

He made it to the vehicle and slowly surveyed the scene, occasionally jumping back from the intense heat and spreading flames. He stopped and looked up at the top of the cliff. "I can't see anything through the fire. And I can't get too close. It's too hot."

"Do you see any signs of escape?"

He looked around for a few more minutes and turned to the man giving orders. "No."

Gloria heard it before she saw it. And she knew exactly what it was; right behind them, a low growling sound, followed by the rustling of bushes. She turned around slowly and there it was, a massive Onza—half-jaguar and half-lion, staring at them with yellowish-red glowing eyes, massive fang-like teeth exposed.

It was twenty feet behind them.

She touched Matt's arm and he turned around abruptly. The Onza growled and, without warning, charged. Matt grabbed Gloria and crouched down, waiting for his life to end, waiting and almost hoping this horrible nightmare would end.

But the Onza leaped over them, disappeared in a hole in the brush, and emerged out the other side in full stride, charging for the enemy.

The soldier stood frozen by the burning SUV, eyes agape, looking fearfully at the incoming threat.

"Shoot it," a man shouted from the cliff.

He opened fire but only got off a short burst of bullets before the Onza closed the distance, sprang into the air, clamped its massive jaws on the soldier's throat and brought him down. He screamed as it tore a massive chunk of flesh from his throat, spit it into the air—as if taunting the men on the cliff firing—and dragged him behind a large oak tree. There, the Onza growled and tore him apart piece by piece, ripping away large chunks of flesh, limbs, even snapping through the man's bones and spitting them into view.

There was a brief silence while the two atop the cliff stopped firing and watched, wide-eyed.

The Onza grew quiet, its prey destroyed.

Esteban's soldiers talked.

"What should we do? Vicente and Rufino are dead."

"Why don't you go down there?"

"I'm not going down there."

"Why don't you go down there?"

"I'm not going down there."

But their decision was quickly made for them.

There was a rustling sound behind the tree where parts of Vicente's dismembered body lay. The Onza suddenly leaped in the air, snarled ferociously at the men, and sprinted up the steep precipice.

They didn't waste any time. They ran to their vehicle, climbed in, slammed the doors and fish-tailed down the dusty road to beat the band.

Had they decided to stay, the band would have played the death march at their funeral.

Chapter Twenty-Four

"What was that beast?" Matt asked an hour later as they marched along a treacherous trail that wound its way up into the mountains.

There had been little conversation to that point, both of them alone with their thoughts, digesting their respective losses, dealing with their grief, mourning, recovering from shock.

Walking ahead of Matt, Gloria stopped, and turned around, facing Matt. She wiped a lone tear from her eye. "It's an Onza."

"Onza?"

"Yes. Half-jaguar and half-lion. They're rarely ever seen, there's no photographic evidence, and some people believe they're just myth, not real."

"So the Onza is to the Sierra Madre what Bigfoot is to the forests of British Columbia?"

She nodded.

"But that wasn't a myth I just saw back there. That was real. That beast saved our lives."

Gloria nodded. "Divine intervention, maybe."

She turned around and they continued walking.

"Where are we going?" Matt asked, after a few minutes of silence.

"My uncle, Romiel Alvarez. He lives a few miles from here."

"Do you have a phone?"

"No, in my purse. In the hospital. You?"

Matt felt a side pocket of his travel pants. The cell phone was there. He stopped, unzipped the pocket and produced it. The screen was cracked and crushed. "It didn't survive the crash."

"At least we did."

"Yeah."

"Any weapons?"

"No. In the SUV."

A sinking feeling of despair settled over Matt as they continued along in silence again. He felt for his money belt. It was there, tucked under his jeans. At least he had money, passport and credit cards. But he didn't know what good they would do in the middle of nowhere. He hoped Romiel had the answers. He knew he couldn't return to Guadalupe y Calvo.

Esteban would be hunting for blood.

And Gloria, for that matter, couldn't return to her house or job. After Jesus's murder of Isidrio, Matt knew enough about drug cartel revenge killings to realize they wouldn't stop until all of Gloria's remaining family and close friends were dead. *What about my family and close friends? Is this ever going to end? That is, unless they think we're dead. That's our only chance. And what about Gloria? I promised to protect her. I don't even know her. I can't keep a promise like that. We're probably still being hunted. What about my own safety?*

Even in his grief, Matt thought Gloria was a gentler, more honest and stable version of her sister, although he had to admit he loved Angelique in spite of her flaws and indiscretions.

Gloria broke the pensive silence. "How did I get out of the burning SUV?"

"I pulled you out."

She stopped again and swung around, staring at Matt with soulful, sorrowful and beautiful black eyes—eyes that reminded Matt so much of the late Angelique. "Thank you. Thank you for saving my life." She hugged Matt tightly and they stayed in that embrace for a nearly a full minute, alone on a mountain trail in the middle of the Sierra Madre, a surreal vista of vast canyons and majestic mountains, a crimson sky and a sliver of an orange sunset visible as it crested a rocky peak.

Misery breeds company. And they both needed the company right now.

They released from the embrace and continued walking.

"No problem," Matt said. "I was just returning the favor. We're even now." As soon as he said it, he realized how lame it came off, like he no longer owed her anything.

"I don't look at it like that."

"Neither do I. It was a stupid thing to say."

Gloria swung around. "Matt, whatever you do, don't do anything for me that you don't want to do. I don't care what you promised Jesus. I won't hold you to that."

"I promised Jesus."

"I don't care. I don't want you doing anything for me that you feel obligated to do. Understand?"

He nodded and they carried on. They arrived at a small stream. Matt sat down on a rock beside the trickling water and Gloria sat beside him. They washed their hands in the water, cupped them together and drank. She tore a piece off the sleeve of her white blouse and dipped it in the water. "Let me clean you up. Your face is covered in blood."

"So is the back of your head."

"Do me, then I'll do you."

"Okay."

She rinsed the torn piece of cloth in the water, wiped Matt's face, cleaned his cut and rinsed the fabric again in the stream before tying it around his head—an improvised bandana-bandage. "There. You look like a warrior now." She offered a half smile, turning the back of her head to Matt.

He tore a chunk of fabric from the sleeve of his t-shirt and repeated the procedure, wrapping the black cotton fabric around her head.

"How does it look?" she asked.

"You've got a two-inch cut on the back of your head and a pretty good-sized lump. But the blood has congealed. How do you feel?"

She shrugged. "I'm okay, I guess. You?"

"I'll be okay. Are we far from your uncle?"

She pointed up the mountain, where the trail became less forested and rocky. "Romiel lives in a cave up there."

"Angel never mentioned him."

"She wouldn't remember him. He's different. Very reclusive. He only wants contact with family, maybe some close neighbors. And those times are few and far between. If he seems a little standoffish, don't worry. It's just a Tarahumara thing. He'll help us, though. He was a shaman, a village leader, before the drug cartels took over the region. All of his family is dead, except for me. Romiel was looking so forward to meeting Angel. Now ..."

Gloria's eyes welled with tears. She stopped and bent down, hands covering her face.

Matt put a hand on her arm. "It'll be okay."

She turned, locking eyes with Matt for a second or two before speaking. "We better go. It's getting late. And cold."

They reached a steep rock cliff with a three-foot diameter black hole about fifty feet up. There were no signs it was inhabited.

Gloria bent down, picked up a small rock and threw it up. It bounced into the small hole, echoing faintly through the canyon.

"Nice shot," Matt said.

"It's in our genes."

The black silhouetted head of a long-haired Indian man appeared and then the tip of a spear protruded from the opening.

"Romiel," Gloria said. "It's me. I'm in trouble."

"Who's with you?" he asked in Spanish.

"It's Matt, Angel's boyfriend."

"Where's Angel?"

"She's dead."

"And Jesus?"

"Dead."

"Move out of the way."

There was a moment's silence before a rope ladder flew out the entrance, dropping to the ground a few feet from the rocky surface where they stood. Matt watched Gloria climb up the ladder and into the cave. Then he did the same.

Romiel pulled the ladder inside. They crawled through a small tunnel and reached a larger opening that was lit by a small fire, the smoke twirling into a hole in the cave wall above it—to where, Matt knew not.

A battered kettle sat on a rusted metal grill perched on some hot embers. Steam billowed out of it. Cooking accoutrements, along with some tin cans, were scattered in a corner near the fire. Some pots hung on sticks protruding from the cave wall. In another corner, blankets and sleeping bags were strewn around, a makeshift bed on the rocks. Beside the bed, there was a pile of clothes, some neatly folded.

After throwing Matt a nod of acknowledgement, Romiel sat cross-legged beside the fire and began a conversation with Gloria in Raramuri, the tribe's indigenous tongue.

Matt understood nothing, so just observed. Romiel wore tattered blue jeans. His bare feet were heavily calloused, bare chest lean and muscular. He had high cheekbones, long black hair held in place by a thin leather head-band, and small, intense black eyes. He had no facial hair and hard lines spider-webbed across his face. Occasionally, as he prepared tea, he would glance at Matt impassively and quickly divert his gaze.

He served tea and prepared bowls of mashed corn, squash and beans, which he handed to them along with some water.

They ate. Through mouthfuls of food, Matt asked: "Do we have a plan?"

"Tomorrow or the next day, Romiel is going into town to see if we're still being hunted and bring back some of my things."

As Gloria and Matt talked, Romiel slipped into a deep, meditative trance. He stared at the dancing flames intently, calmness and tranquility suffusing his being.

"Then what do we do?" Matt asked.

"If Esteban thinks we're dead, you return home and I change my name and relocate somewhere in Mexico. I can't go back to Guadalupe y Calvo now. If they see me, they'll kill me. What do I have there, anyway?"

"What about Romiel? Won't Esteban's men get suspicious if they see him?"

"No one knows he's my uncle, except for Jesus and you."

"So, basically we wait until Romiel returns before deciding on our next step?"

Gloria nodded. "I'm getting tired. I'm going to turn in."

"Me too."

She stood up, went over to Romiel's blanket supply, and returned with two sleeping bags for Matt. He took them and thanked her. She returned to the blanket pile, grabbed two more sleeping bags, and set them down close to the fire, about ten feet from Matt.

They both lay down. Matt glanced at Gloria's eyes, which flickered orange-red in the fire's reflection.

Romiel sat motionless, staring into the fire. His eyes had grown far away.

"Good night," Gloria said.

"Good night."

They were quiet for a time, each alone with their grief and mourning.

Romiel sat meditating, his serene gaze focused on the dancing flames.

Gloria broke the silence. "One more thing."

"What's that?"

"Romiel says Angel and Jesus are in a better place. Death in our religion is not considered an end, but a change. The dead come out at night, and the moon becomes the source of heat and light. Jesus and Angel will be out tonight, watching out for each other."

"Thanks for that, Angel. Sorry—I mean Gloria."

"If you want to contact Angel, talk to Romiel. He can perform a traditional ritualistic healing ceremony. You might see her and find peace."

"Would you participate?"

"Sure."

"Does it involve drugs?"

"Peyote."

"I'll think about it."

After a long silence, broken only by the crackling and popping of the fire, Matt finally felt sleep overcome his traumatized mind. He drifted off and dreamed of murderous carnage: people getting shot, stabbed, tortured, pleading, screaming for their lives to no avail.

One nightmare was vividly clear. He was in an underground parking lot with Gloria and two unknown men. One man's features suddenly darkened. He brandished a knife, explaining that someone had to die, and Matt had to decide who.

"Not Gloria, for sure," Matt said.

"What about this other guy—or you?" the man draped in black asked.

Out of nowhere, another man appeared in the parking lot. Matt looked at the frightened "other guy" and remembered. He had met him earlier in the nightmare and, although the details were vague, a conversation had started, one that had ended on friendly terms. Could he call the man a friend? No.

He hardly knew him. But did he like him? Yes, he seemed like a nice guy. *It's him or me.* Finally after many protestations and pleas, which went unanswered by the killer, Matt said: "Okay, him then. Kill him."

The man begged and pleaded for his life. "No, not me, please don't kill me. I want to live. Please don't kill me. I don't want to die."

But the killer dragged him into a corner of the parking lot as Matt and Gloria watched, horrified. The killer stabbed him multiple times, each puncture punctuated by another cry for help. Just before the man expired, he had been reduced to a blubbering, sobbing idiot.

"Don't kill him. I'm sorry. Kill me. Kill me," Matt pleaded. He woke up sweat-soaked and trembling with fear.

Chapter Twenty-Five

"So much killing," Gloria said. "What would be considered lawlessness anywhere else is the law around here. But I guess that's the way it is, the way it will always be."

Matt had just explained his chilling nightmare to Gloria. They sat side by side on a boulder beside a trickling stream in the forest a short distance from the cave. It was a postcard-perfect sunny afternoon; thick forest, a blue sky dotted with thick white cumulous clouds, majestic mountain peaks, vast canyon vistas, birds chirping, even a beautiful woman to converse with, Matt thought. But the undercurrent of death that coursed below the surface was unnerving. Matt had been particularly rattled by the nightmare. He'd woken in the middle of the night, terrified, wondering where he was, heart thumping madly in his chest, cold terror permeating his body.

So, after waking, drinking tea, and eating a bowlful of beans, he and Gloria had decided to take a small hike while Romiel went into Guadalupe y Calvo. The middle-aged Tarahumara descended the ladder behind Gloria and Matt, extracted a climbing pole hidden in some bushes, and pushed the ladder back into place before returning the pole to its hiding spot. Then, without a word, he had disappeared barefoot down the small trail, running with slow and measured strides.

Matt was trying to make strides of his own by learning the meaning of the nightmare. He had just admitted that it would be unusual for him to choose to die in favor of someone he barely knew. It was new to Matt, something foreign to his personality that he wanted to understand.

Gloria had responded slightly off topic by talking about the lawlessness—actually, the law—of the Sierra Madre.

"In some ways, I admire it," Matt said, somewhat surprised by his own response. "People don't fuck with you if they understand the repercussions. It's not like an eye-for-an-eye justice at all. That would be if someone kills my sister, I kill them. But this is nothing like that. It's if they steal something from me, I kill them, a head-for-an-eye justice. But, to get back on topic, what do you think the murder in my nightmare means?"

"I don't know. Maybe it's a sign you're beginning to think less selfishly or something. I don't know you well enough to say for sure. Maybe you're not selfish at all."

"I am. I chase money like it's the most important thing in the world."

"That's not good. Our traditional beliefs say you can't prosper with material things. Your success is measured by your ability to grow food and your willingness to share it with neighbors, not by how much money you make or how many toys you accumulate. That means nothing to us. Our traditional economy is based on ... believe it or not ... corn beer and random acts of kindness. Instead of money, the Tarahumara trade favors and large containers of the homemade brew."

"That's admirable. And, although in many ways your culture is getting destroyed, it still perseveres."

"Many have tried to conquer us and failed. But the Tarahumara are tough. We defend our culture and families through a passive resistance, withdrawal into inhospitable terrain, and avoidance. But when things get nasty, we get nasty."

There was a moment's pause while Matt digested the information. "But your culture is under constant attack?"

Gloria nodded. "Look at me, forced to work as a waitress in a raucous cantina full of rapists, killers, drug-smugglers. I'm losing my cultural identity. Romiel is the only person I have to remind me of it."

"I admire him. He has nothing, but has everything."

"He's got a big heart, and he's well-respected by other Tarahumara for his wisdom and powers of healing," Gloria said. "He still gets consulted, still performs ritualistic healing ceremonies. He's also a ferocious warrior."

"He's a little standoffish where I'm concerned."

"Don't take it personally. He'll warm up to you. He doesn't extend trust automatically. You have to earn it. And he's a little xenophobic when it comes to foreigners. You know, once bitten, twice shy. But with him it's more like a thousand times bitten. Have you thought about a peyote ceremony, by the way?"

"I don't know. My mind is a little fucked right now. I think for that kind of thing one has to be of stable mind and body. I've got a lot of shit spinning around in my head. I'm still smarting from all the death. I'll think about it, though. What about you? Are you going to do it?"

"I've done it before, and it's an eye-opener. I'll do it if you do it, how's that?"

"Okay. Did you tell Romiel about the Onza?"

Gloria nodded.

"And what did he say?"

"He said it's a sign."

"A sign of what?"

"Of more bloodshed and death to come."

A sudden rustling in a nearby bush startled Matt.

Gloria reached for a handgun Romiel had provided. Romiel might be all about preservation of traditional Tarahumara culture, but he wasn't beyond keeping a few guns around the house—especially in the Wild West.

The Onza poked its massive head out from the brush, snarled and stared at them with yellowish-red eyes.

They froze, fixing their eyes on the predator.

Then Matt moved to stand up.

"No," Gloria whispered. "I don't think he means us any harm."

Against his better judgment, Matt sat back down on the boulder by the stream and watched, trying unsuccessfully to still a pounding heart. He was cognizant of a slow and subtle change taking place in him. *Fear. It's a fucking waste of time.*

Gloria set the gun on the rock. The Onza watched them for a long moment, eyes focused like a knowing predator about to destroy an unknowing prey.

After e moment, they averted their gazes, unwilling to tempt fate.

This is it, Matt thought, trembling. *We're dead this time. This fucking nightmare is over.*

But the legendary cat suddenly relaxed, sat down on all fours and began licking its paws, seemingly oblivious to its new human companions.

"See," Gloria said. Her voice had risen from the earlier whisper as her confidence grew. "He likes us. He's our protector. I think Jesus sent him."

Slowly, Matt's heart rate returned to normal as he pushed the fear into small compartments of his mind and locked them. At that moment, he wanted more than ever to throw away the keys.

Gloria was calm, almost meditative, as she studied the Onza. After a few minutes, they resumed a conversation about the culture and customs of the Tarahumara.

As they talked, the Onza occasionally glanced up at its companions in a non-threatening way. A nearby bird cawed and startled the Onza. It leaped up suddenly, spun its head around, and darted into the bushes.

"Goodbye, El Diablo," Gloria said.

"El Diablo?"

"That's what I'm going to call him. El Diablo, for the most part, is good according to our beliefs. He just misbehaves sometimes. In fact, he's God's brother ... I like it. El Diablo."

Chapter Twenty-Six

"El Diablo," Matt said the following evening, eyeing the silver necklace with a snarling Onza, red eyes glowing eerily. They were sitting cross-legged around a small fire in the cave, and Romiel had presented Matt with the gift.

"If that's what you want to call him," Romiel said in Spanish. "He's for your protection."

"Thank you." Matt stared at the ornamental Onza, wondering if it was a talisman that possessed magical powers. *You never know around here.*

The shaman nodded, pulling out a matching Onza necklace and handing it to Gloria. "El Diablo," she said. "For our protection. Thank you."

They put them on each other while the shaman waited patiently. He had returned from Guadalupe y Calvo about an hour ago, effortlessly carrying about 120 pounds of supplies. He had briefed them on the situation in the small town. Hospital staff, local police and many residents had fled. There was a bloody battle underway between rival cartels, and people were being executed—in some cases tortured and decapitated to send a message. It was believed the Mexican army was moving in to quell the violence.

According to Romiel, Esteban believed Gloria and Matt were dead, and had called off the hunt. Although Romiel added a footnote: "With the drug cartels, you can never be sure."

Romiel had visited the gravesites of Jesus and Angelique, who were buried in a small cemetery just outside of town, side by side, small white wooden crosses marking their respective resting places. He had performed a ritual blessing ceremony, insuring safe passage for Angelique and Jesus into the afterlife.

Now he prepared for another ritual—a peyote healing ceremony. He stirred the large pot beside the fire and acknowledged the participants. "It's ready. Are you ready for the sacrament?"

They nodded.

"I want to warn you," the shaman said. "Peyote is a window into the spiritual realm. It can transform you. It allows communion with spirits. It gives power, authority, guidance, and healing. The healing may be emotional or physical, or both. You may experience terrifying visions. Remember, I'm here to guide you, to help you through them, and to eliminate evil, should it surface. Is that clear?"

"It is," Matt said.

Gloria nodded.

Romiel continued. "After your traumatic losses, you both need healing, guidance and transformation into a higher plane of existence. You need to find peace with the souls of Jesus and Angelique. Let's begin."

There was a small leather mat on the ground beside the boiling peyote tea. On it sat a sword, a cross, two burning candles, a decorative ceramic pot of water, and a large quartz stone. The sword symbolized the powerful force they would need to drive out evil, the water was fluidity of motion, candles represented the healing light of the afterlife, and the quartz stone was a symbol of the clarity of vision they were about to experience. Every shaman ritual differed to some degree.

This was Romiel's healing ritual.

Outside, the night was black and still, the moon full and ominous. Millions of stars glittered.

Romiel began pounding on a deerskin drum while humming a ritualistic ancient chant. After a few minutes, he stopped, stirred the tea, lit a corn-husk-wrapped cigar, exhaled a cloud of smoke into the boiling peyote and handed the cigar to Matt. Matt took two drags and handed it to Gloria, who took a puff before passing it back to Romiel.

Romiel poured peyote tea into tin cups. He handed one to Matt, another to Gloria. "Drink when I tell you." He lifted a ceramic jar of crushed peyote powder. He passed it to Matt, instructing him to swallow two tablespoons of the powder, wash it down with peyote tea and pass it to Gloria.

Sitting cross-legged in front of the dancing flames, they repeated the ritual three times while Romiel beat the deerskin drum and chanted.

After a few minutes, Matt felt calmness settle over him, a surreal feeling of inner peace he had never experienced before. Then a blue hue suffused the room and a kaleidoscope of brilliant colors suddenly emerged, wild dancing geometric patterns of dazzling brilliance and depth. The dancing flames grew and transformed into ... no, it couldn't be, but it was ... the ferocious Onza floating above him, growling menacingly, reddish eyes penetrating his soul and spreading unimaginable pain and fear through his body and mind.

The shaman chanted and beat the drum.

Matt tried to scream, but found he could not. He shielded his eyes but it didn't help. The Onza drifted closer until soon gigantic reddish eyes were all he could see. Suddenly the pupils turned black—an abyss of pain, death and suffering.

He shuddered at the images of death that materialized like a dark collage; machine-gun fire, people screaming in terror, dying en masse, being tortured, decapitated, slashed, burned—all manner of unspeakably brutal, cold-blooded murder.

Angelique's death flashed before him, accompanied by a needle-like incision to his heart. Then Jesus's murder and another stab of pain to his heart, accompanied by a blood-curdling scream from Gloria. *Is she seeing the same visions?*

Matt leaned over and vomited inside a small bucket Romiel had provided. *Purge. Purge the evil.* The vomit was ... *no, no, no* ... the dark red color of blood.

But the pain precipitously vanished and was replaced by a feeling of ineffable wellness. A thought entered his mind. *The Onza. The Onza is our protector.*

The chant stopped.

The drumbeat stopped.

He felt Romiel's reassuring hand on his arm as he continued vomiting blood into the bucket. "Steady, my brother. The evil will pass."

He brought his gaze to the dancing flames. The cave walls disappeared and he could see the twinkling stars, brilliantly glowing full moon and an incredible display of color rocketing across the night sky.

He stared at the heavens, transfixed by the overwhelming feeling of wellness and oneness with nature and the gods.

Gloria screamed again and vomited into the bucket. Romiel was at her side instantly, offering words of comfort, driving out the evil forces.

A bluish-gray image slowly emerged in the night sky. Matt felt his heart rate quicken as it became clearer and he realized who it was. The face glowed radiantly and beautifully beside the brightly shining moon. "Angel," Matt said. "It's you."

Her lips didn't move, but he heard her calm voice. "It's me, my love. And I'm at peace." Angel smiled down at him.

Then Jesus's face emerged in the heavens, calm and serene.

"Jesus," Gloria said.

"I love you," Jesus said. "I am in the afterlife with Angel. I'll protect her. We're okay."

Gloria smiled. "I love you, Jesus."

Jesus's gaze swept over to Matt. "Look after her. Please."

Matt nodded, was about to speak, but then another image arose. The moon transformed into the head of the Onza. But it wasn't growling anymore. It was grinning—its abyss-like black eyes boring into Matt's soul.

Angel lifted a hand and placed it gently on the Onza's head.

Jesus patted the beast.

It purred, a soothing roar that reverberated through Matt's entire being, flooding him with calmness and purpose.

******

But then another image appeared and Matt felt raw terror course through his veins. He didn't know how he knew, but he knew. It was Esteban, approaching from behind, grinning wickedly, pointing an AK-47 at the three images in the dark sky.

"No, no, no," Matt said. "Behind you."

But it was too late. A staccato-burst of machine gun fire pierced the still night air.

The images of Jesus, Angel and the Onza disappeared and were replaced by a blood-red curtain of death and blood-curdling screams.

And something else—a ringing sound, starting off low in intensity, but then reaching a debilitating crescendo—a cacophony of high-pitched, ear-splitting rings. Matt covered his ears and screamed into the night: "Ahhhhhhhhhhhhhhheeeeeeeeeeeeeeee ... help me!"

Epilogue

"Help, me ... help me," Matt shouted. He opened his eyes suddenly and realized he was on the floor of his Vancouver apartment—he had fallen out of bed again. And it wasn't night. It was morning.

He wondered when the recurring nightmare would disappear.

The phone was ringing.

He gathered his thoughts, slowly picking himself up. He was drenched in sweat. His pounding heart slowly returned to a steady rhythm approximating normal.

It would have to do.

He answered, recognizing the number. "Sal?"

"Matt, it's almost eleven. You're late."

"Sorry. I had a late night. Give me fifteen minutes."

"I have your paperwork ready. It arrived early."

"Thanks." Matt hung up the phone.

Showering, he thought about the nightmare, sighing in relief after he realized it was not how the actual peyote healing ceremony six weeks ago in the Sierra Madre had ended. No. It had ended with the confidently calm faces of Angel, Jesus, the Onza, and the overwhelming feeling of inner peace.

And purpose.

Matt didn't fully understand the twisted ending in his nightmare, but it was the second time it had haunted his psyche. *It probably just means I have more work to do—miles to go before I sleep.*

And he *had* traveled miles before escaping from the Sierra Madre. He had survived in Romiel's small cave for a week before an escape vehicle had been arranged. He had hiked to a small Tarahumara Indian village where El Toro's soldiers had driven him into Juarez. From there, he crossed the border into El Paso by taxi and boarded a plane to Vancouver.

He stepped out of the shower, toweled dry and admired his new look. He was lean and muscular, the result of frequent visits to the gym. His once-long hair was cropped neatly into a brush-cut. He also sported a goatee, a new set of veneers on his teeth and a pair of what he liked to call John Lennon glasses.

He dressed quickly and left the apartment, walking the five or so blocks. The rain of the last few days had given way to sunshine, and it cheered his soul as he stepped into the elevator of a high-rise office building a few minutes later. He headed to the 12th floor, where his friend Sal ran an efficient legal firm.

Inside the office, he sat down and Sal regarded him curiously, not for the first time since his return home.

"It just seems awfully coincidental, that's all," Sal said, after they dispensed with social niceties.

"What's that?"

"You know what I'm talking about. And you, too—you're different."

"I feel better than ever."

Sal sighed, regarding Matt with some annoyance. "When are you going to level with me? Joe Andreas, the courier who was suing you, mysteriously drops the lawsuit after his house was broken into and he was assaulted. Rod Badrickis, the property manager who was suing you, drops the lawsuit after someone blows up his car and he almost dies. Do you know he's still in the hospital, recovering? He'll never walk again. And serious disfigurement from burns. And what about Rick Folly, the property manager who sued you in civil court and pressed charges in criminal court for harassment? I hear he's locked in a padded room in a loony bin with a straitjacket. But, before going bat-shit crazy, he dropped all the charges."

Matt shrugged. "They got what they deserved. Maybe I have someone looking after me? I told you about the peyote healing ceremony."

"I don't buy any of that shit. And that's not even the kicker. Detective Ben Lyons decides all of a sudden you're not a suspect in the murder of Alex Liberty, and wants nothing to do with questioning you."

"I told you. He found new evidence pointing to a guy called Rod Vermooth."

"What new evidence?"

"How should I know? I told you I'm innocent."

Sal sighed. "I hope one day you *will* tell me. I'm your friend. You can trust me."

"I know."

"What're your plans now?"

"I don't know. Work for a while. Maybe take a trip. I'm not sure yet."

Sal opened a drawer to his desk and extracted an envelope. Handing it to Matt, he eyed him cautiously. "Remember, don't say a word about where you got this."

"Don't worry. I'm loyal to a fault. You know that."

"It should give you some protection from Esteban's drug cartel."

Matt opened the envelope and examined the fake identification. *Michael Onza. I like it.* "Thanks. It's just a precaution. I'm sure I'm fine."

"Guess I'll have to start calling you Michael."

"Guess so."

"I'm just curious. Why'd you pick the surname Onza?"

"The Onza is to the Sierra Madre what Bigfoot is to BC forests—a mysterious beast that's fiction to some, fact to others, depending on what you believe. Either way, it's a legendary cat. I like that. The Onza is also known as a fierce predator. I like that, too."

Sal shook his head. "I don't understand the new you. But I'm starting to put some of the pieces together. Maybe one day I'll have the full picture."

Michael stood up, walked to the office door and winked. "Maybe one day I'll tell you. Have a good day. Talk to you soon."

******

Outside, he stopped at a Western Union office, wired some money, bought a plane ticket at a travel agency and returned home, where he called his secretary, Michelle.

"Hi Matt. I mean Michael. Sorry. That's going to take a little getting used to. I have to tell you, the phone is going crazy. I can't believe how you've turned the business around in such a short time."

"This is a new era for us. I'm glad you're happy. Listen, I was thinking. Remember that woman, Julie, who was in severe financial distress and needed to sell her home?"

"Julie Macklebie. How could I forget? Her ex tried to kill her with a pickup truck and supposedly murdered her grandfather. He's still under investigation."

"Have you heard from Julie lately?"

"She just called again yesterday. Claims no other realtors will take the listing. She sounded desperate."

"Do me a favor. Call her and set up an appointment. Tell her we'll help her."

"Are you serious?"

"Dead serious."

******

Later that evening, Michael gazed out his apartment window at the full moon in the distance, smiling, knowing the mysterious forces of the afterlife—and the Onza—were shining upon him. A feeling of peace washed over him and he had an epiphany of sorts. Since returning from the Sierra Madre, he had struggled to find the meaning of the nightmare he had had while sleeping in Romiel's small cave.

But, suddenly, as clear as the glowing white moon, it struck him. *The underground parking lot. Having to choose who dies. Picking someone, then at the last minute, saying no, kill me, kill me.* It was suddenly crystal-clear. It was a premonition dream, foretelling he would overcome his fear of death. He initially thought it was something about being less selfish, but now he knew the real meaning.

And he had to tell her.

He picked up the phone and dialed Gloria Alvarez. But she was no longer Gloria Alvarez. She had changed her name to

Angelina Alvarado. She answered the phone from her rented beachfront condo in Nueva Vallarta, Mexico. Since his return, Michael had been sending her money regularly.

She answered. "Hi ... Michael."

"Angel, how are you?"

"I'm well. And you?"

"Everything's coming together." Michael explained the epiphany. "Remember you thought it meant that I was becoming less selfish?"

"Yes."

"But that's not all it meant."

"Oh. What else?"

"I'm not afraid of dying anymore. Jesus and Angelique taught me that. The dream told me that. The peyote ceremony taught me that. The Sierra Madre taught me that."

"I'm so happy you're growing as a person. I hope you come and visit someday."

"I bought a plane ticket today."

"Really," Angel said. "When are you coming?"

"I leave in two weeks. I'll email the details."

"That's great. I'm looking forward to seeing you."

"Me too. I just have a little unfinished business to take care of first."

There was a moment's pause.

"Best of luck with it," Angel said.

Michael brought his hand to the silver chain around his neck and looked at the ominously glowing red eyes of the ornamental Onza. "We have the Onza to protect us, remember?"

"Of course."

"There's something else."

"You're full of surprises."

"When I arrive, I would like to take you out on an official date. I'm growing very fond of you. Are you okay with that?"

"I'd love to."

Michael looked at the clock. It was time. "I have to go. I'll call you tomorrow."

"Be careful."

He hung up, grabbed his jacket and left the apartment. After walking eleven blocks, he arrived at a small low-rise apartment building. He ducked behind it. He waited exactly four minutes and the main-floor door opened.

Rod Vermooth cautiously looked both ways and stepped out into the night.

Michael glanced around. Seeing no one, he checked his belt and felt the cold comforting steel of the combat knife. He was doing it because he knew Detective Lyons was restricted by the confines of law, and many more victims would likely die before justice could be served. He was doing it for El Toro. He was doing it for Jesus. And he was doing it for Angel, the troubled but kind and loving soul residing in heaven.

It's what they would have wanted.

He was no longer afraid to die, no longer afraid to kill.

And he was no longer Matt Green. He was Michael Onza, a brave and fearless warrior whose job it was to serve up justice Sierra Madre style—A Head for an Eye.

He allowed Vermooth a block head start before he stepped away from the building and walked briskly up the street. By now, Michael had memorized the lyrics to Lou Reed's song, *Fly Into The Sun*. He hummed its tune, grinning with the satisfaction of a knowing predator pursuing an unknowing prey.

> *I would not run from the blazing light*
> *I would not run from its rain*
> *I'd see it as an end to misery*
> *as an end to worldly pain*
>
> *An end to worldly pain*
> *an end to worldly pain*
> *I'd shine by the light of the unknown moment*
> *to end this worldly pain*
>
> *And fly into the sun*
> *fly into the sun*
> *I'd shine by the light of the unknown moment*
> *and fly into the sun*

As he plunged the blade deep into Vermooth's back, a single thought occurred to Michael Onza:

This isn't murder. It's self-defense.

The End

Selected Bibliography

Richard Grant. *God's Middle Finger*. New York: Free Press, 2008.

Christopher McDougall. *Born to Run: A Hidden Tribe, Superathletes, and the Greatest Race the World Has Never Seen*. Vintage, 2009.

Carlos Mario Alvarado Licon. *APUNTES SOBRE EL PENAL DE GUADALUPE Y CALVO 2004*. Chihuahua, Chihuahua, Mexico, 2004.

Bernard L. Fontana, with photographs by John P. Schaefer. *Tarahumara: Where Night is the Day of the Moon*. Tucson, Arizona: University of Arizona Press; 2nd edition, 1997.

Carl Lumholtz. *Unknown Mexico: Explorations in the Sierra Madre and Other Regions, 1890-1898*. New York: Dover Publications, 1987.

J.G. Kennedy. *Tarahumara of the Sierra Madre: Beer, Ecology and Social Organization*, Alington Heights, IL,: AHM Publishing, 1978.

Peter Nabokov. *Indian Running: Native American History & Tradition*. Sante Fe, NM: Ancient City Press, 1981.

Also by William Blackwell

Phantom Rage, Poison Rage, Infected Rage
Nightmare's Edge
Resurrection Point
Brainstorm
Rule 14
Assaulted Souls
Assaulted Souls II
Assaulted Souls III
Blood Curse
Black Dawn
The Strap
The End is Nigh
Orgon Conclusion
Freaky Franky
The Witch's Tombstone
The Dark Menace
Tales of Damnation
In Your Dreams
Macabre Alley
A Head for an Eye

Tales of Damnation Preview

"These were a very enjoyable set of imaginative short stories that had lots of variety to keep readers guessing what would come next." -Amazon

If you enjoy a nail-biting roller-coaster ride through hell, you'll love Tales of Damnation, a collection of terrifying short horror stories.

The Spot: Watch a school bully finally get his comeuppance in grisly fashion.

The Cab Ride: Witness a malignant narcissist realize a little too late that it's time he started caring.

Fire and Fury: Feel the heat when a pyromaniac learns that playing with fire also means getting burned.

The Succubus: Discover the horrifying consequences when a down-and-out man succumbs to the seduction of a succubus.

Fake Friends: Learn the shocking difference between real friends and fake friends.

The Stalker: Ride shotgun with a demented stalker as she tracks her prey through the haunted woods.

And there's more. A total of thirteen finely crafted short horror tales guaranteed to educate, terrorize, and entertain.

Take a wild ride to hell and back. Get your copy today.

About the Author

Canadian dark fiction author William Blackwell studied journalism at Mount Royal University and English literature at The University of British Columbia. He worked as a journalist and a newspaper editor for many years before pursuing his passion for storytelling. His novels have been characterized as graphic, edgy, and at times terrifying. Currently living on a secluded acreage on Prince Edward Island, Blackwell finds much of his inspiration from Mother Nature, odd people, traveling, and bizarre nightmares.

Author Comments

Thank you for reading this book. I would be eternally grateful if you would post a book review on your favorite book retailer website. A positive review is the highest compliment a writer can receive. Reviews are crucial to the success of any author and they also help readers discover new books. You don't have to say much. A few sentences will suffice.

In other news, I have a gift for you. Complete the signup form below with your name and email address and download a FREE copy of *Resurrection Point*, a dark tale about the horrifying consequences of experimenting with death and resurrection. You're only agreeing to be kept up to date on blog posts, new releases, and freebies. I promise I won't spam you and you can unsubscribe at any time.

Thanks again for your support.

http://www.wblackwell.com/free-ebook/